"Marry you?"
Trista breathed

For one ecstatic moment her heart soared like an eagle. One glorious moment, before it all came back. Then, almost hysterically, she gasped, "No! I can't marry you!"

Dylan watched her for what seemed endless moments. "You just can't?" he said finally. "Don't I deserve some explanation?"

Trista stared at him. "You have to ask me that? After you and she.... You even told me I reminded you of her."

He took a couple of steps across the kitchen. "Trista, what on earth are you talking about?"

"My mother!" she shouted. "The divine Angela! When you were making love to me you were remembering her. Dylan, you were my mother's lover!"

These books may be available at your local bookseller.

For a free catalog listing all titles currently available,
send your name and address to:

Harlequin Reader Service
P.O. Box 52040, Phoenix, AZ 85072-2040
Canadian address: Stratford, Ontario N5A 6W2

The Ashby Affair

Lynsey Stevens

Harlequin Books

TORONTO • NEW YORK • LONDON
AMSTERDAM • PARIS • SYDNEY • HAMBURG
STOCKHOLM • ATHENS • TOKYO • MILAN

Original hardcover edition published in 1983
by Mills & Boon Limited

ISBN 0-373-02608-0

Harlequin Romance first edition March 1984

CHAPTER ONE

THE sporty lines of the metallic silver-grey Mazda RX7 catapulted along the narrowish highway with what seemed to be breakneck speed and the driver, tall and dark-haired and undoubtedly competent, consciously made an effort to ease his foot on the accelerator and the car slowed considerably. Only twenty or so kilometres to go, he told himself. There was no dire hurry.

Forcing himself to relax, he glanced around at the passing landscape and to his surprise he found he was experiencing a sensation akin to *déjà vu*. It was much the same sort of feeling he had when he re-read a favourite book after a couple of years to find it just as enjoyable, just as appealing on second reading.

The familiarity of the surrounding scenery flooded over him, rolling back the ensuing years with ease. With an indecent ease, he thought wryly, when you bore in mind that over thirteen years had gone between. My, how the time does fly! And it's been such fun, he mocked himself.

Looking around him dispassionately, he supposed the countryside was too hot and dry for most tastes, as dry as the proverbial limeburner's boot, and it was somewhat desolate for the most part, the predominant colours rusty reds and dusty beiges, with the occasional stark grey, white and black of a skeletal tree. But, overlaid by the deep cobalt blue of the cloudless sky, it took his breath away.

This central southern part of Australia, the Eyre Peninsular, was hardly everyone's idea of a land of beauty, but it caught him somewhere on a vulnerable nerve and moved him more than he could have imagined it would. Much of the land about him was relatively poor quality and the rainfall variable, but he knew the area still managed to produce more than a third of the state's wheat.

He flexed his tired muscles. It had been a long drive, in more ways than one, some six hundred and fifty kilometres from Adelaide, skirting Spencer's Gulf along a coastline that was mostly sand dunes, changing as you moved inland to undulating plains of saltbush and mallee and gently rising hills. South Australia, a manmade wilderness, many called it.

No, not everyone's cup of tea, he thought, but for him it formed the backdrop of his childhood years, the abstract part he'd carried with him since he'd left, never all that far from his thoughts in those thirteen years.

Now the prodigal returns. A cynical smile tightened his face again.

He had passed the airport now and entered North Shields, and then there was the bay. The water was as blue as he'd remembered it was, and he slowed the car, drawing to a halt in a layby. The engine idled almost silently and he slowly reached to switch it off, climbing out of the driver's seat with some reluctance, walking around to the passenger side. Folding his arms across his chest, he leant his long body against the car. The stiff cool breeze lifted his dark hair from his forehead and the sun beat down on him.

One hand went automatically to rub the dark growth of beard that disguised his face. He'd be glad to shave it off, he reflected absently, while his eyes, shaded by dark-lensed sunglasses, made a sweep of the scene before him.

One of Australia's most spectacular harbours, the arc of Boston Bay curved to make a lake of sparkling turquoise velvet. Three times the size of the famed Sydney Harbour, the bay was protected from the Southern Ocean by the six and a half kilometre length of Boston Island.

He felt as though he knew every indentation, every plant and rock of that shoreline. There was the skirt of light sand on the foreshore, the strip of green lawn, the Norfolk pines in front of the shopping centre, the smaller town jetty berthing two fishing boats. Further around were the huge concrete cylinders of the grain silos and Brennens Jetty, the new one, surely longer than he remembered, reaching out into the bay like a huge green-backed centipede.

Shading his eyes, he could pick out a couple of bulk grain carriers at the large jetty ready for or in the process of being loaded while another huge ship was anchored awaiting a berth. A couple of yachts with multi-coloured sails tacked across the bay's surface while others bobbed on their moorings in the sheltered water to his right. All in all it was a scene more picturesque than you would see on any postcard.

A hundred screaming memories tossed about in his head, and although the growth of dark beard disguised his facial expression his dark eyes were coldly cynical.

Home. Where the heart is. Home. Where his

heart was broken. A sound split from him, a sharp self-derisive laugh. He was starting to sound like an escapee from a penny dreadful. A broken heart? You have no heart, he told himself, you never had one.

Almost irritatedly he strode back around the car and slid into the driver's seat, they drove purposefully on, passing a sign that welcomed him to Port Lincoln, Tunarama City.

'Where are you off to?' The voice came from the patio above and Trista stopped and smiled up at her sister-in-law.

'Just for a walk down to the shore and back. I've been cleaning the flat, going all domestic, and I need some fresh air. Want to come?'

'No, thanks. I'll stay here with my feet up.' Joanne patted her tummy. 'I've got a good excuse. Doctor's orders until the baby's born.'

Trista frowned. 'There wasn't anything wrong, was there? I mean, you are okay?'

'Yes, I'm fine. Don't you go worrying, love. Ray does enough worrying for the three of us—four, counting His Nibs,' she grinned.

'You're sure?' Trista asked.

'I'm sure. I just get tired quickly. And I'm a bit fed up waiting. These last weeks are going to go slowly, I can feel it in my bones.' Joanna shifted carefully on the lounger. 'Why don't you take Frank with you for company?'

At the sound of his name the large brown dog of dubious parentage sat up and panted expentantly.

'Okay,' Trista grinned. 'Come on, Frank!'

The dog bounded excitedly down the stairs.

'What a name for a dog! You'd think your husband could have picked a more dignified name like Rover or Spot. But Frank!' Trista raised her large hazel eyes skywards.

'You know Ray,' replied Joanne. 'Or you should—he was your brother long before he was my husband.' Joanne laughed. 'Besides, he does look like a Frank, you must admit.'

Trista rubbed the dog's ears. 'We couldn't call you anything else now, could we, boy?' She waved a hand at her sister-in-law. 'See you later.'

Heading towards the blue waters of the bay with the dog trotting beside her, Trista sighed. She couldn't help but worry about Joanne, who was more like a sister than simply her brother's wife. Joanne wasn't having an easy time with her pregnancy, and she'd waited so long for this baby.

Trista's brother Ray, ten years her senior, had met Joanne in Adelaide and they had been married for nearly seven years. They had all but given up hope that they could have a family and had even started discussing applying for adoption when Joanne discovered she was pregnant, so their baby was desperately and eagerly wanted. If anything happened to the baby or Joanne . . .

Trista pushed the thought from her mind. It didn't bear thinking about. But she still couldn't help worrying about them. After all, Ray and Joanne were the only family she had. Trista had only been sixteen when their father died and Ray and Joanne had moved back into the Vaughan family home. Family stuck together, Ray said.

By the time Trista had finished her schooling and been taken on in a junior secretarial capacity with a local firm of solicitors she had suggested that perhaps Ray and Joanna would prefer to be on their own. Ray wouldn't hear of his young sister moving out, but just over a year ago they had compromised. The small granny flat beneath the large old home had been renovated and Ray had grudgingly agreed that Trista live in it. She was close enough to set his mind at rest about her wellbeing, and it gave Ray and Joanne the house to themselves. It had all worked out perfectly.

Trista reached the gravel road through the scrub that led down to the shore. She had tied back her shoulder-length light brown hair into a ponytail at her nape, and as she followed the track, turning out of the relative protection of the low windblown bush the brisk breeze from the open bay tossed her hair about, separating a couple of strands from the elastic band that held it in place. The strands streamed across her face and she pulled them back behind her ear, smiling to herself as she stood on the shore overlooking the bay and Snapper Rock, a natural granite slab which was used as a launching ramp by local boat-owners.

Frank excitedly chased a group of seagulls who fluttered upwards with unhurried disdain. Thrusting her hands into the front pockets of her shorts, Trista took a deep breath of the sharp clean air, expelling the breath with slow enjoyment.

If her two weeks' holiday in Adelaide with Joanne's family had done one thing for her it had reminded Trista how much she loved this area, how much she missed it when she was away. Not that she hadn't appreciated having the short break in town. She'd been rather run down after a bad bout of 'flu and Joanne's mother had spent the whole two weeks cosseting and 'feeding Trista up', as she put it. And Trista felt so much better for it. But it was good to be home again.

A couple of fishing boats made their way across the bay and Trista's eyes followed them as she tried to pick out which boats they were. Not the *Shelly Star*, she knew, as her brother wasn't going out for a few days yet.

And that was a worry, too. Albeit her brother hadn't said anything, she had a feeling Ray was more than a little disturbed about his fishing business. He had inherited the *Shelly Star* from their father and although they had had a couple of lean years tuna-wise he had been extending himself financially, negotiating to buy another boat, *Blue Dancer*.

Unfortunately, on the verge of settling the sale, the owner had died and now Ray was waiting to hear if the new owners were interested in selling the boat. *Blue Dancer* had been sadly, criminally, Ray said, neglected over the past couple of years and, according to Ray, grossly mismanaged by the hired skipper.

Ray's boat was his life. He had been on the *Shelly Star* with their father since he was old enough to hold a fishing line and a fisherman was all he had ever wanted to be. To see a fine boat like the *Blue Dancer* in the state it was at the moment was to Trista's brother nothing short of sacrilege.

Frank trotted up with a piece of stick in his mouth and dropped it at her feet, wagging his tail, shaking his whole hindquarters in anticipation, and Trista smiled at him throwing the stick for him to chase.

Tyres crunched on the gravelly road surface behind her and she gave the sleek grey car an incurious glance before turning back to the view of the bay. She was absently aware of the closing of a car door, but the car was unfamiliar to her and apart from that she didn't make a habit of talking to strangers, wasn't really used to mixing with many people apart from Ray and Joanne. She preferred to keep to herself. Touching no one and no one touching her. It was safer that way.

So the fact that she might have had company didn't occur to her until a deep voice just behind her made her jump and swing around.

'Sorry.' His lips moved upwards, showing a flash of strong white teeth surrounded by a dark beard and moustache. 'I didn't mean to startle you.' His eyes too were hidden behind brown sunglasses, the lenses catching the reflection of the water.

Trista's head was back as she looked up at him. He must be well over six feet tall and he dwarfed her five foot five. 'That's all right. I just wasn't expecting anyone to be there, that's all,' she said rather stiltedly as her eyes skimmed over him.

Being so tall, above average height, he could have looked gangling, but he didn't. He was well built, broad-shoudered, narrow-waisted, long-legged. His dark denim jeans were tailored, moulding his hips and muscular thighs and his white loose-weave shirt emphasised the tanned well-developed biceps of his arms.

The sight of the distinctive Pierre Cardin monogram on the shirt for some inexplicable reason stirred a spurt of irritation in Trista, although exactly why it should do so she couldn't have explained. He had every right to exude success, she tried to tell herself. Her boss, Trent Hardie, also dressed well and she had never held it against him. What reason could she possibly have for singling out this prosperous, very authoritative-looking stranger? So he wore expensive clothes and drove a flashy car. So what? He was most probably a tourist anyway.

Trista turned back to pat Frank as he dropped the retrieved stick at her feet. Then the dog gave a little whine as though he couldn't decide whether he wanted to investigate the stranger or plead to have Trista throw the stick for him again.

The dark man reached over, patted the dog and rubbed his ears, before picking up the stick and tossing it, sending Frank barking enthusiastically after it.

So much for Frank, my intrepid guard dog! Trista thought wryly.

'What's his name?'

Trista's eyes rose to meet the dark glasses in enquiry.

'The dog.' He indicated with an inclination of his dark head.

'Oh. It's Frank,' she replied, and a deep chuckle rose from the man's chest, the vibrant, blatantly masculine sound touching a nerve deep inside Trista, and she shifted uneasily.

'Frank,' he repeated, amused, and she felt a faint smile lift the corners of her mouth.

'He's my brother's dog and he insisted he looked like a Frank. We couldn't change his mind, so Frank he is.'

'You live around here?'

She nodded. 'Just up the road.' She could feel his eyes behind the dark glasses move over her and she felt a flutter in her breast, as though her heartbeats had faltered and then raced away. 'Where are you from?' she heard herself ask him, taking herself by surprise.

'Queensland,' he replied after a pause, and turned slightly to gaze out over the bay. 'How's the fishing?'

'We're hoping for a good season.' Trista followed his gaze to the two boats now small spots on the afternoon blue of the bay. 'Last season wasn't all we'd expected it to be because of the bad weather. January and February were pretty grim, but luckily most of the boats had a late run of catches that made some difference.'

'Your family owns tuna boats?' he asked.

'Yes.'

Before Trista could elaborate a large four-wheel-drive towing a fibreglass half-cabin cruiser appeared along the track, and Trista and the stranger turned to watch the vehicle swing around, preparing to back down the ramp to launch the boat.

A familiar fair-haired figure climbed out of the passenger side of the Range Rover and as she recognised him Trista's lips tightened. The young man caught sight of her and paused. Immediately Trista called the dog and turned towards the track.

'Just a minute.' A strong tanned hand reached out and clasped her arm, his flesh cool on her warm skin, and she shivered slightly, her eyes darting to the stranger's face and away again, her face growing hot.

'Could you use a lift?' he asked casually.

'No, thank you—I must go.' His fingers still held her and now her flesh burned where he touched her, starting the same tingling sensation in the pit of her stomach. She looked up at him wishing she could read the expression in his eyes behind the disguising glasses. 'Goodbye,' she managed to get out huskily.

Slowly he released his hold on her and she moved away from him, all instincts warning her loudly that she should flee from him, with all haste, for her own peace of mind.

At the top of the track she paused to catch her breath before walking on a little less vigorously up the hill. She'd done it again—she'd shied away from human contact like a cautious colt. Anyone would think she was a bashful teenager, not a supposedly mature twenty-one-year-old. There must be some quirk in her character that caused her to shun people, to back away from any form of personal overture outside of her family and a few close friends. She'd tried to overcome it, come to terms with herself, but without success.

And seeing Troy Aimes hadn't helped. Even now she could cringe with shame recalling that episode over six months earlier. Looking back, she still couldn't explain why she had accepted his invitation to take her to dinner. She should have known better. Hadn't she learned an equally painful lesson when she first arrived home from boarding school?

Obviously she hadn't, she reminded herself. And it hadn't hurt any less this time than it had the first time it had happened.

At seventeen, her schooling finished, she had put a tentative step into the world of the group of youthful Lincolnites. For Trista, who was basically rather shy and introverted, it had taken some considerable self-determination. Her experience that first time, at such a vulnerable age, had sent her even further into her shell, and no coaxing or encouraging from Joanne and Ray had convinced her to go out and try to meet young people her own age, meaning young men. But of course she had never told them about that disasterous time with Chris Jones.

Trista's lips twisted ironically. Chris Jones was now a married man with a young child and she doubted he'd even remembered the evenings he had spent with her. Four years later she had let down her guard again, only to have history repeat itself.

Troy Aimes, tall, fair-haired, very good looking, the son of a local businessman, was considered one of Lincoln's most eligible young bachelors. He was a couple of years older than Trista, and she had met him one warm Saturday afternoon out on the Sleaford Bay road. She was about to change a flat tyre on her small sedan when Troy's Manx beach-buggy pulled over and he had smilingly offered his assistance.

He seemed pleasant and easygoing right from the start, and with her tyre changed he had introduced himself, chatted for a while, and then they had parted. A few days later he had phoned her and asked her out to dinner. Reluctantly she had accepted.

In the next few weeks Troy had been all she could have wished for in an undemanding companion. He was interesting and amusing and attentive without being pushy, his goodnight kisses were light, asking nothing of her. And Trista's defences had relaxed. With the advantage of hindsight she could see he had played her as skilfully as any master fisherman and she, fool that she was, and lonely, had taken the bait, hook, line and sinker.

Inside her flat she took a quick shower, wrapping herself in a bath towel as she padded across the bedroom to collect fresh underclothes. Pausing before her full-length mirror, she ran critical eyes over her all but nude body. Her legs were reasonable, she admitted, and her slender form was filled out in all the right female places. In fact, she was just an average looking twenty-one-year-old woman, she decided, pulling her hair loose from its rubber band.

Then why can't you act like a twenty-one-year-old woman, she asked herself, instead of a naïve, skittish, timid adolescent? What was it in her make-up that made her afraid of any sort of relationship? Because she could admit that she was afraid, afraid of the same pain rejection brought.

It had always been that way with her. When she felt someone moving closer she turned and ran with almost panic-stricken speed. It was a form of self-preservation, she told herself.

The face of the dark bearded stranger swam before her and she paused, shivering again at the remembered sensations of his fingers firm on her arm. She had run from him too, but somehow her flight from the stranger had been, in some inexplicable way, quite different.

Standing in the small boutique where she often bought her clothes, Trista frowned at the rack of dresses. You're a typical Libran, she told herself exasperatedly. Give yourself a choice of more than one and while you try to make a decision you flounder around for hours like a stranded whale! Sighing resignedly, she held up the two dresses to show the assistant before she walked into the changing cubicle to try on the both of them.

And now it will be even harder to choose, she thought wryly as she pulled off her loose peasant style blouse and wrap-around skirt and slipped the cool crêpe of the blue sleeveless dress over her shoulder, smoothing it over her waist.

The pale shade seemed to suit her and she twisted around to look in the full-length mirror behind her. Was it a little too casual for work? Trent liked her to be well groomed and look the part of private secretary to an up-and-coming solicitor.

She stepped out of the blue dress and into the lemon one. The colour lightened her fairish brown hair. Mousey, Trista called it, not recognising that the sun-streaked softness of it, coupled with her easy tan and large hazel eyes in a face that was wistfully attractive, rated more than a cursory glance.

Outside in the shop there were sounds of more prospective customers entering, the grating slither of hangers sliding along racks, the murmur of voices. The walls of the fitting room were paper-thin and as the two girls walked closer Trista could overhear their conversation, and she listened absently, if inadvertently, without realising she was doing so.

'How about this one, Rose?' asked one female voice.

'No, that's not exactly that I was looking for,' was the reply. 'I want something with a tinge of green in it if possible. Otherwise I'll have to get new accessories.'

'Rosie! Joy! Hi there, you two!' called a third, more strident voice. 'I thought I saw you duck in here.'

'Hello, Gay. Got the afternoon off?' asked Joy, her voice bright and young sounding.

'No such luck. I'm on an errand for the boss, so I can't stay long. Are you looking for something for the wedding next week?'

'Mmm. I don't know what I want, but I will when I see it,' laughed Rose. 'Have you got your outfit yet? Joy's got hers.'

'Yes, I'm collecting it on Tuesday.'

Trista unzipped the lemon dress and replaced it on its hanger, deciding to take it in preference to the blue one.

'I suppose I'd better get back.' Gay went to move off. 'Hey, I nearly forgot. You'll never guess who's coming back to Lincoln!' She paused for effect. 'Never in a million years of guessing!'

'Well, who is it? Come on, Gay, don't keep us in suspense,' cried the younger girl.

'Of all people, Dylan Ashby, that's who!' delivered Gay in a triumphant tone.

Trista's gasp was drowned out by the other girl's question.

'Who's Dylan Ashby?'

'Who's——? Who's Dylan Ashby, she asks?' Gay's voice rose in disbelief. 'You mean you haven't heard of Dylan Ashby?'

'No, I don't think so,' replied Joy.

'Have a heart, Gay,' came Rose's voice. 'Joy's only a chicken compared to us, and it was years ago now. It must be, what,' she paused to consider, 'good grief! It has to be all of twelve or thirteen years ago.'

'Is it that long? I suppose it must be. Seems like just yesterday,' said Gay. 'Wow! Didn't it cause a furore?'

'What did? What furore?' asked Joy impatiently. 'Now you've got me all curious again.'

'You must have heard someone mention the biggest scandal in the town? My God, everyone was talking about it for ages afterwards!'

'Gay, the poor girl was barely at school,' Rose half laughed. 'And besides, it's pretty much a case of water under the bridge, so who really cares now? It was so long ago most people have probably forgotten all about it anyway.'

'You haven't. I haven't,' stated Gay. 'And I'll bet there's a fair percentage of the female population who haven't forgotten. The divine Angela wasn't too popular. From what I gleaned at the time no one's man was safe from that femme fatale.'

'What femme fatale? Angela who, for heaven's sake?' demanded Joy eagerly.

'Angela Vaughan. You know, Trista's mother.' Gay replied. 'What a scandal, with a capital S! Everyone, but everyone, knew about the Ashby affair.'

CHAPTER TWO

'ASHBY? But I thought you said her name was Angela Vaughan.' Joy sounded confused.

'It was.' Gay sighed loudly. 'She married Dave Vaughan. He died a few years ago. He was years older than Angela. Then she fell for Dylan Ashby and they ran off together. She was old enough to be his mother, too!'

'That wasn't quite true, was it?' asked Rose.

'Yes, it was. Dylan Ashby was in my brother's year at school, so that makes him, let's see, about thirty-one now. Ray Vaughan, Angela's son, was also in that year, so as I see it, it makes Angela Vaughan old enough to be Dylan Ashby's mother,' finished Gay.

'Crikies! I'll bet there was a to-do about it,' remarked Joy. 'Even in these liberated old times there'd be rumblings of distaste.'

'From what I've heard,' continued Gay, 'Angela was always out for the main chance. Dave Vaughan had just bought his own fishing boat when Angela started batting her eyelashes at him. She was the eldest of that prolific King family from up Koppio way and even at seventeen she was no better than she should be. Everyone was really surprised when Dave Vaughan married her. She always reckoned Ray was a premature baby, but—well, it sounds like it was her story, etc., if you get my drift.'

'Gay, come on, that's a bit steep!' Rose put in.

'There's no need to go into all that. Ray Vaughan's a friend of my Bill's and from all accounts he's a nice guy. I've always found him to be anyway.'

'That's as may be.' Gay wasn't to be put off.

'Where's Angela Vaughan now?' asked Joy. 'I mean, I always thought Trista's mother was dead. Trista's never said she wasn't.'

'I don't know. She could be. But who'd own up to having a mother like that? Anyway, no one's heard any more of her or Dylan Ashby since they ran off together. And now he's coming back!' Gay couldn't keep the excitement out of her voice.

'What's this Dylan Ashby like? Why all the fuss? You're just about drooling, Gay,' laughed Joy. 'Have a crush on him or something?'

'Why all the fuss? You must be joking! Every female between six and sixty was head over heels in love with Dylan Ashby way back then, even if he was only a teenager. He was gorgeous, the dreamboat of the school—tall, dark, and so-o-o handsome. Wasn't he, Rose?'

'I guess he was,' Rose agreed reluctantly. 'But not as nice as my Bill.'

'He must still be handsome, the way you're going on,' Joy remarked, 'or is he over the hill?'

'Over the hill?' spluttered Gay. 'He's only thirty-one!'

'Is he still as nice-looking?' asked Rose, laughing at Gay's indignant expression.

'I don't know—haven't seen him yet. But I'll bet he is. His sort of good looks go on for ever.'

'When did he arrive?' asked Joy.

'He hasn't as far as I know. I only got the info

yesterday from old Mrs Green who heard it from Elsie Jenner who said Dylan's Aunt Jean Parker told her he was coming home, I guess because of his father's death. And by the way, young Joy, that's enough of the "over the hill" bit. Dylan Ashby is part of *my* generation and I consider myself to be in my prime. What do you say, Rose? Aren't we at our peak?'

'What? Oh, sorry, Gay, I was just thinking.'

'What about? Dylan Ashby?'

'No. About Ray Vaughan and his sister,' said Rose quietly. 'How will they feel seeing Dylan Ashby again? It can't have been a very happy time for them, and this is going to bring it all back.'

'That's for sure!'

'Poor Trista, I feel sorry for her,' began Rose.

'She can look after herself, believe me,' remarked Joy.

'That sounds ominous.' There was a note of spiteful glee in Gay's voice. 'Something tells me you don't much care for Trista Vaughan.'

'I think she's stuck up. She never talks to anyone and—well, it's not exactly that, but—oh, just forget it,' Joy finished irritatedly.

'She's always seemed very nice to me,' observed Rose. 'Just quiet. Maybe she's simply shy.'

'Not shy enough to turn down Troy Aimes when he asked her out. She led him on and then dropped him. Probably because he wouldn't marry her,' Joy added cattily.

'Oho—that's it!' Gay laughed. 'So young Troy Aimes is behind it? Are you still carrying a torch for that young playboy, Joy? I thought you were over that.'

'He isn't a playboy,' began Joy defensively.

'Goodness, look at the time!' Rose put in placatingly. 'I have to collect the kids from school.'

'And I guess I should be getting back to work before the boss realises I'm not behind my desk. Sorry for pulling your leg about Troy Aimes, Joy. I guess I'll see you both at the wedding.' Gay added as they began to move off, 'Wonder if Dylan Ashby will be there. Wasn't he a friend of the groom's way back, Rose?'

'I don't know,' replied Rose, 'but it would be pretty short notice to add him to the guest list at this late date.'

'Suppose so. Pity, though—I'm looking forward to renewing my acquaintance with the dashing Dylan Ashby. See you both.' Gay left the other two at the door of the boutique and headed in the opposite direction.

Trista moved her frozen muscles at last to sink down on to the chair in the change cubicle, clutching the lemon dress unconsciously in her arms.

It couldn't be true. Dylan Ashby couldn't possibly be coming back. Dylan Ashby—after all this time! Pain surged up inside her and she gulped a deep steadying breath as she tried to gather her shock-scattered wits into some order.

Did Ray know? No, he couldn't know, or he would have told her himself, said something.

Dylan Ashby here! How dared he? The pain now took second place to a surge of pure anger. How could Dylan Ashby have the absolute gall to show his face in Lincoln again?'

Trista bit her lip. It would all start over once

more. His presence would rake it all up and people would talk, stare at her furtively, whisper behind her back the way they used to do when she was a child. And Ray—surely it would be worse for him. After all, Dylan Ashby had supposedly been Ray's best friend.

Slowly Trista dressed in her own clothes, took the lemon dress to the assistant at the counter and paid for it. Had the girl heard that conversation too? Was there a tinge of pity in the woman's eyes? No, don't start it, Trista, she commanded herself. Don't start imagining things before they begin to occur. Like one pursued, she bolted for home and the sanctuary of the four walls of her flat.

'Hi, Joanne!' Trista forced a smile on her face as she put her head around the open kitchen doorway.

'And hello to you. Come on in.' Joanna looked up from the vegetables she was washing and wiped a loose strand of fair hair back from her face with her arm. 'Staying to dinner?' She asked.

'Only if you sit down and let me do the cooking,' Trista said firmly. 'But as a small concession I'll let you do the directing.'

Joanne gratefully relinquished the potato peeler and sank on to a chair. 'Thanks, love. I am a bit tired this evening.

'What were you planning on having?' Trista asked as she deftly diced the fresh carrots.

'Grilled tuna steaks—plain for me, with tartare sauce for you and Ray. I've got the fish marinating ready to be grilled, so there's just those vegies to do.' Joanna sighed as she put her feet up on the chair opposite her.

'What time are you expecting Ray?'

'Any time now.' Joanne glanced at the wall clock. 'He rang about half an hour ago to tell me he was hungry enough to eat five horses and that I'd hear him coming by his tummy rumblings!'

Trista laughed. 'That's my brother! We never could seem to fill him up.'

'I wouldn't mind except that I only have to glance at a meal and I stack on the flab, and yet Ray's just a ball of solid muscle. It hardly seems fair, does it?' Joanne grimaced.

'Joanne! Love, I'm home.' Ray Vaughan's boots tattooed on the stairs and he strode into the room. 'How's my favourite girls? Hi, Tris!' He slapped Trista on the bottom as he crossed to kiss his wife on the cheek. Pulling a chair alongside hers, he rested his arm about her shoulders.

There was little family resemblance between Trista and her brother, for he was dark-haired and brown-eyed like their father. And like their father he was big and muscular, his skin tanned by his hours spent in the sun.

'Mmm, something smells good. Have I got time to have a shower before the food's served?' he asked.

'A shower, Ray Vaughan, is a necessity, I'd say.' Joanne pointed to his shirt. 'Engine oil and plain old dirt I can identify, but what, pray, is that?'

Ray grinned. 'Tomato sauce, actually—slight accident with my hamburger at lunch. But not to worry.' He patted her on the cheek as he headed for the bathroom. 'My wife uses Brand X, guaranteed to remove the sturdiest stain,' he laughed as he left them.

'He's very jovial tonight,' remarked Joanne happily as she began to set out the cutlery.

Trista turned to place the tuna steaks under the griller, guiltily wishing she didn't have to bring up the subject that had been bombarding every corner of her mind since she had overheard that conversation in the boutique that afternoon.

Apart from the initial dreadful time all those years ago she had never discussed the subject with her brother, so she had no real idea how he felt about it. After all, she had only been eight years old at the time, tearful, confused and very insecure. All she seemed to remember was clinging to her brother, not understanding when he told her that her mother, that beautiful creature who always smelled of flowers, had gone away. And the one time she had questioned their father he had angrily pushed her aside and disappeared into his room, leaving her frightened and bewildered. Only later, as she grew older, had the understanding come.

The same quivering uncertainty niggled at her stomach and she hastily turned the tuna steaks under the griller, basting them with the marinade to keep them moist. How was she going to tell Ray?

'You're quiet tonight, Tris,' remarked Ray as she dished up the dessert.

The 'right' moment for her to mention to her brother the gist of the conversation she had overheard just hadn't presented itself through dinner.

'You're not feeling sick, are you?' frowned Joanne concernedly.

'Oh, no, I'm fine—really,' Trista assured her.

'I know what it is—the thought of going back to work on Monday,' grinned Ray.

'Well, it will be a bit of a drag after two weeks of rest and recuperation, but I guess I'll get used to it again.' Trista swallowed. 'But there is something else I'd like to talk about.' She stopped, searching for the right words.

'What's up, Tris?' Ray prompted gently. 'Come on, out with it!'

'I overheard something when I was shopping this afternoon and I—well, I don't know if you've heard about it.'

Ray raised his eyebrows enquiringly. 'About what?'

'I don't know how to tell you,' Trista twisted her spoon unconsciously in her hand.

'Tell me what?' Ray was still smiling at her. 'Spit it out, Tris.'

'I overheard someone say that Dylan Ashby was coming back.' She watched her brother apprehensively.

Ray's easygoing expression faded, his lips thinning into an angry line. 'The hell he is,' he muttered.

'Ray?' Joanne turned worriedly from Trista to her husband and her hand went out to touch his arm. 'Ray, what is it? Who's this, who did you say, Trista?'

The scowl deepened on Ray's face and he set his fork down beside his half finished slice of apple pie. 'Dylan Ashby,' Ray said quietly, then seemed to gather himself together. 'Who told you, Trista?'

'Well, no one, exactly. I just overheard some people talking.' Trista knew it would do no good to mention the people involved.

Ray drew a deep breath. 'Dylan bloody Ashby! He's got some nerve coming back here! You know, when old Bill died it did cross my mind that Dylan might inherit his estate, seeing as Pete was killed, but I didn't think that ba—— that he'd have the audacity to show his face hereabouts.'

'Ray, who is he? What's he done?'

Ray swore softly as his wife glanced from Trista's paleness to her husband's anger. Trista's eyes fell to her plate.

'Well, who's going to tell me?' she asked firmly.

Ray sighed and ran his hand through his hair. 'He's old Bill Ashby's younger son,' he told her a little more composedly. 'He was at school with me. We were best mates as kids, grew up together. Until he showed his true colours. My God, I could have killed him with my bare hands at the time!' He wiped his hand along the line of his jaw and across his chin as though trying to force himself to relax.

'But, Ray, what did he do?' Joanne persisted.

'Do? Dylan Ashby turned bloody gigolo and ran off with our dear sweet sainted mother, that's what he did!' Ray bit out aggressively.

Joanne gazed open-mouthed at her scowling husband and a thick silence stretched between them.

'I always thought your mother was dead,' Joanne said softly at last.

'She is dead as far as Trista and I are concerned,' Ray remarked flatly.

'When did—well, how long ago did it happen?'

'Thirteen years ago.' Ray's lips thinned.

'Trista was only eight years old!' he added angrily.

'And you haven't seen her since then?' Joanne directed her question at Trista, but before Trista could more than shake her head Ray spoke.

'Trista hasn't, but I have.'

His words brought Trista's head up in surprise. 'You've seen our . . . her?' she mouthed incredulously. 'But when?'

'About seven years ago, before Jo and I were married.' Ray shrugged and then his eyes fell from something he read in his sister's expression. 'Look, forget it, Tris. I'm sorry I mentioned it. I didn't mean to, but I guess this has really rocked me.'

'You can't ask me to simply forget it now,' Trista said sharply. 'When did she come back, Ray, and why didn't you or Dad tell me about it?'

'Tris!' Ray ran his hand distractedly through his hair. 'Let's just leave it.'

'No, Ray. I am supposed to be part of this family, aren't I?' she asked. 'I have a right to know. She was my mother, too,' she added, unable to keep the thread of hurt from her voice.

Ray sighed and patted her hand. 'You're right. I'm sorry, Trista—we should have told you. She came back to try to pick up where she left off with Dad, but he was having none of it, and sent her packing.' He glanced at the paleness of his sister's face and his eyes fell again. 'You were away at school and Dad and I—well, we saw no need to upset you. We didn't want to rake it all up again.'

'Then your mother broke up with Dylan Ashby?' asked Joanne gently.

'I guess. How could it last anyway? She was old enough to be his mother, damn it all!' Ray said grimly. 'And who knows how many more there were between Dylan Ashby and when she came crawling back to Dad. She had some nerve expecting our father to forgive and forget after what she did to him!'

'Perhaps she just realised she'd made a mistake,' began Joanne.

'A mistake? Humpf! The biggest bloody mistake of her life,' Ray scowled. 'No, don't try to whitewash her to me, Joanne. She didn't give a tinker's damn for what she was leaving behind, and I can't forgive her for that. So as far as I'm concerned she can go take a long walk off a short jetty. And she can take Dylan Ashby along with her.' Ray pushed his half-finished dessert aside and stood up. 'Can I leave the dishes with you two tonight? I'm going to read the paper.'

Joanne turned her sympathetic gaze on Trista as Ray left the room and without a word the two girls began to clear the table.

'Trista! How are you feeling?' Trent Hardie's kindly face was wreathed in smiles as he beamed at her.

'Fine, thanks, Trent,' Trista smiled back. As bosses went, she thought for the umpteenth time, Trent was the best.

'All over the 'flu now?'

She nodded. 'Thank heavens. I didn't realise one tiny 'flu bug could take so much out of me.'

'That's for sure,' Trent agreed. 'You have to look after yourself, you know, it wasn't much fun here without you,' he smiled.

'So I see,' she motioned to the heap of folders ready to be filed away, and Trent gave her a sheepish grin.

'I didn't want to upset your system by putting them in the wrong places.'

'You're forgiven,' she told him easily, 'but two weeks off is going to make all this a bit hard to take.'

'Well, just don't go overdoing it,' Trent frowned concernedly. 'It's waited two weeks, so a few more days aren't going to bring things to a standstill.'

His pale blue eyes were passing that same message and Trista's gaze fell to the files in her hands. He touched her arm lightly, almost reverently. 'Great to have you back, Trista,' he said softly as he disappeared into his office.

'Oh, Tris—nearly forgot.' Trent's sandy fair head reappeared. 'I've got an early appointment this morning, so send him in as soon as he arrives.'

'All right.' Trista bent down on her haunches to the lowest drawer in the bright green cabinet. Thank goodness there weren't too many T to Z's. She sighed softly.

Well, back to work. It was as though she hadn't been away. The office was still the same, its autumn tonings highlighted by the bright green modern office furniture.

And, of course, Trent was still the same. She smiled faintly. Trent would always be the same— even-tempered, unassuming, reliable, his main aim in life being to project a suave, trustworthy image of a successful, dependable solicitor.

Eight years ago Trent had joined old Mr

Turnbull, himself part of the town for longer than Trista could recall, and four years ago the older man had added Trent's name to the firm: Turnbull and Hardie. It was then that Trista had been taken on as Trent's secretary, a very junior secretary, and right from the beginning they had established an easy working relationship.

That Trent wanted that good working relationship to continue into their private lives Trista was quite well aware, but she had always held back on that count, not really sure it was what she wanted. She liked Trent very much, realised that as a person there were few as kind, as solid, as likeable, but . . . There was always the 'but', and Trista had no desire to place any strain on their working association by stepping into a more personal relationship, one she might regret. Trent Hardie was far too nice for that.

She couldn't exactly put her finger on what actually held her back. He was pleasant, if not wildly attractive-looking, his thin fair hair and colouring making him look a little boyish, much to his annoyance. He was thirty-four, she knew, and to offset his somewhat youthful appearance he combed his hair rather severely and wore it short back and sides. To look too young, Trent believed, did not invite confidence from his clients.

Although he was not quite six feet tall he was well built, inclined to stockiness, and she knew he played a better than average game of squash and was the opening batsman of a local cricket team. He was also a member of the local branch of Rotary International and attended church regularly. All in all, he was a very reputable member of the community and she should have jumped at the chance of going out with him, but . . . There was that word again.

Perhaps her reticence was caused by something inside herself, that same part of her make-up. Maybe she would never find anyone she could lower her guard with, could trust.

A faint niggle of depression gripped her and she tried to shake it off. It wasn't that she was looking for a fantastically handsome Adonis. For some obscure reason, unsolicited, she thought of the tall dark stranger who had appeared when she was walking the dog, and she shivered. Ruefully she admonished herself. Who was she trying to kid? A girl did not just pick up with a stranger she met on the beach. He was simply a ship that passed in the night. No more.

Trista grimaced as she filed in the last folder and stood up, reaching for the next stack. The phone rang and she answered it, balancing the handpiece on her shoulder as she continued her filing. The call was for Trent, and switching it through she replaced the receiver.

'Good morning.' The deep voice behind her made her start and the top few folders slid to the floor.

She swung around to face the newcomer realising that the sound of the phone must have drowned out the closing of the office door. She automatically reached for the fallen files.

'Please, allow me,' he said, amused, and gathered the folders at his feet, handing them to her.

'Thank you.' Trista's voice husky in her ears, not sounding anything like her own. But he was by far the most attractive man she had ever seen.

Dressed in an immaculate dark grey suit with what was obviously an expensive pale blue silk shirt, he could have stepped from the pages of a glossy fashion magazine. A rush of colour washed her cheeks as she fumbled with the files she held. And somehow he appeared familiar to her.

'I seem to have developed the habit of frightening young women. You're the second in a few days,' he smiled driving interesting creases in his smooth cheeks, the corners of his eyes, deep brown-black eyes, crinkling at the corners.

Trista felt a teasing sensation grip her, turning her legs to unsteady jelly. She gazed back at him in amazement. Could he be the same stranger who had appeared behind her when she had been walking the dog? But the dark beard and the moustache ... This man was dark-haired and tall, but clean-shaven.

Large in her face, her eyes met his and a flicker of something that could have been shock passed over his strong features. Trista felt herself go hot and then cold all over.

'Good God!' he ejaculated faintly, almost absently, as though he had been looking into the past. 'I'm sorry. I——' he paused and shook his head, 'you reminded me of someone I used to know,' he finished softly, and his eyes travelled over her face, seeming to disect each feature. 'The likeness is there, and yet it's not.'

At that moment Trent's door swung open and he stepped into the outer office. 'Thought I heard voices. Come on in.' He held out his hand as the taller man approached. 'I'm Trent Hardie.' Trent smiled his solicitor's smile. 'And you must be Dylan Ashby.'

CHAPTER THREE

DYLAN Ashby. Dylan Ashby! That name was starting to haunt her. And that the tall bearded stranger—for that was who the man undoubtedly was—and Dylan Ashby should be one and the same was a cut that went unwarrantedly deep.

With the dark beard shaved off he was . . . He was what? Trista asked herself harshly, a mixture of sensations surging through her, passing over her like a tide of destruction. She was hurt, disappointed. Attracted, and yet repulsed.

There was no denying he was tall dark and handsome. Very handsome, jeered an inner voice, handsome enough to be the cause of the quickened erratic beating of her heart in her breast.

Well, he'd have to have been reasonably good-looking for her mother to have noticed him. Why else would a mature woman run off with a teenage boy leaving her husband and family behind her?

Trista sank down on to her chair. Her mother and Dylan Ashby. How could she find anything even slightly attractive about a man who had known, known in the biblical sense, her own mother? She felt a wave of nausea rising in her like bile to choke her and tiny beads of perspiration prickled her brow.

Time seemed to flow about her as she gazed sightlessly at the now forgotten files. What was he doing here? What business could Dylan Ashby have with Trent Hardie?'

But of course! She closed her eyes and gently massaged her temples. Dylan Ashby would be here to discuss his inheritance. With the death of his elder brother Dylan would be the sole heir to Bill Ashby's estate. That involved the large old house almost diagonally opposite the Vaughan home and the fishing boat, *Blue Dancer*, the boat Ray had been negotiating to buy.

Now Ray would have to approach Dylan if he still wanted the fishing boat, and Trista knew he did want it. Why, all of a sudden, did Dylan Ashby's life have to be so closely aligned with theirs? Especially after what had happened.

Poor Ray! He had been waiting so long already for old Bill Ashby to make a decision about the sale of the boat. Now there would have to be more discussions, and Ray wasn't going to like dealing with Dylan Ashby of all people.

On the other hand, Dylan Ashby might be really keen to sell the boat. After all, he had never shown any interest in fishing before. According to her brother that fact had been a continual abrasion between Dylan and his father, Bill's insistence that Dylan take over *Blue Dancer* and Dylan being just as adamant that he wanted no part of the tuna fishing industry.

So perhaps he was only here to sell up the estate before moving back to wherever he'd come from. Queensland, hadn't he said? Well, the sooner he rejoined his banana bender friends the sooner everything could settle back to normal.

The intercom buzzed and Trista jumped her hand shaking as she reached across to depress the switch.

'Yes?' Her voice came out sounding strangely stilted.

'Tris, how about some coffee?' Trent asked brightly.

'Of course. I won't be long.' She sat back and gathered herself together. It wouldn't do to let that hateful man know she was disturbed by his presence.

The coffee-maker was switched on all day as Trent drained cup after cup and Trista set out two chunky locally made pottery mugs on a tray. Taking a deep breath, she tapped lightly on Trent's door and went inside.

'Ah, coffee,' smiled Trent, taking the cup Trista presented to him. 'You haven't met Dylan, have you, Tris?' he asked, totally unaware of the spark of tension that seemed to be multiplying between the other two.

It was all Trista could do not to snatch her hand away as their fingers touched when she passed him his coffee.

'Dylan Ashby, my secretary, Trista Vaughan,' introduced Trent.

'On the contrary, we're old neighbours from way back, aren't we, Trista?' Dylan was standing now, and smiling, and his dark eyes seemed to burn where they touched on her.

Trista's body was tensed as she faced him and she tried to fight down the awareness she felt rising inside her, an awareness she had never experienced before with any man. Her smile was a faint lifting of the corners of her mouth and she could tell by the slight hardening of his own expression that he was not unaware of her lack of enthusiasm.

'One of my most vivid memories is of Trista

falling out of a tree and landing at my feet.' His eyes watched her with a burning intensity.

'I remember falling out of the tree,' Trista said rather pointedly, and now a small frown of puzzlement gathered on Trent's brow at her tone. 'And I recall breaking my arm,' she added lightly.

'You mean you've forgotten my manly deed?' Dylan laughed softly and the deep masculine sound had Trista's stomach quivering like a jelly.

She raised her eyebrows questioningly.

'I carried you in my arms up to the house while Ray rang for the doctor. Don't you remember?'

'No, I'm afraid not.' Trista put the sugar bowl on the desk beside him.

'Tsk, tsk!' He shook his head. 'My best act of gallantry, and now the lady doesn't remember,' he said teasingly, his eyes moving over her face in that same probing way before he smiled again. 'But as you were only knee-high to a grasshopper at the time I'll forgive you, Tris.'

'Thank you,' she heard herself say drily as she began to walk across to the door.

'Trista—just a minute.' Trent's voice reminded her with a shock that he was still there, her boss, and that she was at work. Damn Dylan Ashby! He had totally upset her whole equilibrium.

'Dylan's now the owner of the *Blue Dancer*,' Trent was saying. 'I would have liked to have taken him down to meet the man his father left in charge, but I have to be in court in,' he glanced at his wrist-watch, 'just over half an hour. Do you think you could take him down?'

'But the *Blue Dancer* is at sea, isn't it?' Trista blurted out, horrified at the idea of being alone with this man.

'Came back yesterday,' smiled Trent, once again not conscious of the atmosphere that to Trista filled the room. 'We won't be much longer, just a couple of loose ends to tie up.'

'I'm sure Mr Ashby doesn't need me to find the *Blue Dancer*.' Trista wasn't going to give in easily. 'He probably knows the wharf area like the back of his hand.'

'Don't you want to take me down to the boat, Miss Vaughan?' His voice was deeply sensual with a trace of underlying mockery at her formality.

She swallowed, her heartbeats thundering in her chest as his dark eyes warred with hers. To her complete self-derision she had to admit she was not immune to him, that by some crazy quirk of fate she was attracted to him and his solent maleness.

'I'm sorry, I have loads of work to catch up on,' she began.

'Nothing that can't wait, Tris,' Trent broke in. 'Give us a few minutes and then you can be off.'

'But what about the phone? Someone should be here to answer it.'

'That's why we've got the answering service,' Trent smiled. 'I'll switch it on when I leave.'

'All right.' Trista left the office to return to her own. How on earth was she going to face taking Dylan Ashby down to the pier when her whole attitude demanded that she tell him exactly what she thought of him?

But that only added to her uncertainty, because it was becoming increasingly difficult to clearly define those wayward thoughts. In actual fact there was a full-scale war going on inside her and she reluctantly admitted that her good intentions were suffering rather formidable losses.

'I suppose you'll notice a difference in the town,' she said as the battle died away with her quietly spoken words. Keep it light, she told herself forcefully. Don't give him the satisfaction of knowing he was causing her this turmoil. Don't let him get to you. But that was a lot easier said than done when he was sitting so close beside her in the confines of the luxurious silver Mazda, heading along the foreshore.

'I wouldn't have believed it of the old home town,' he agreed. 'And of course you lose a little of the perspective over the years.'

They fell silent and Trista swallowed quickly as her throat constricted painfully. How could he put what he'd done into any sort of perspective at all?

'The silos seem larger, for instance,' he remarked as he drew the car to a halt at the stop sign before the railway sidetrack to the huge cement grain storage cylinders on their left.

Trista found it impossible to answer him and they moved off slowly to the car park. Dylan didn't immediately open the door and rested his arms lightly on the steering wheel as he gazed at the scene, the hustle and bustle of the huge bulk loading jetty.

'This is where I see the most change,' he said reflectively. 'Probably because the bay was so much a part of my childhood. I always seemed to be here, fishing, swimming, boating.' He turned his dark eyes on her. 'But I guess I don't have to tell you that. You've probably done the very same things growing up here too.' He smiled at her and deep creases ran down his cheeks bracketing his mouth.

Trista had to drag her eyes away from that mouth before she was mesmerised. Those curving lips were far too sensual, too inviting. Her childhood was something he had wreaked havoc on, too, and she clenched her hands together in her lap.

'Actually I didn't spend very much of my childhood here.' She kept her voice flat for fear of showing him too much. 'I was sent away to school when I was quite young.' Her eyes met his levelly and she couldn't quite suppress the flash of anger that rose from inside her. Going away to school came with the departure of her mother.

Dylan's own gaze clouded just a little, but he made no comment as he turned and climbed out of the car, walking around to hold the passenger side door open for her.

The tangy sea breeze whipped Trista's hair back as it was lifting white caps on the choppy surface of the bay, and she raised her hand to wipe a wayward strand from its trail across her face.

'The boat will be along the other side,' she told him, hoping that no one would notice her with Dylan Ashby, and she began to walk quickly across to the pier proper. What a field day the gossips would have if it got back to them! Trista Vaughan seen with Dylan Ashby, the man who ran off with her mother!

As usual the area was a hive of activity, fishermen, sightseers, workmen moving back and forth. A large eight-wheeler transport was unloading pallets of bags on to the first boat and an empty semi-trailer rattled over the uneven surface, returning for another load of sacks of grain for one of the two huge bulk carriers berthed further along the jetty. High steel web arms reached across from the conveyor belt to run grain through pipes into the hold of the other ship.

They walked past a number of vessels, both prawn and tuna boats, dwarfed by the size of the grain carriers. It wasn't unusual for there to be in excess of ten million dollars' worth of fishing boats bobbing beside the jetty.

A number of hands working on the deck of one boat eyed Trista quietly before their gazes shifted to Dylan. As she was Ray's sister they all knew her, but they were also aware that she kept to herself, so there were none of the usual calls some of the other local girls might have come to expect.

Trista slid a sideways glance at Dylan and she knew those dark eyes weren't missing much. He turned slightly away from her, his attention caught by one of the newer prawning boats, and she studied his profile.

It was strong and masculine, she was left in no doubt about that, with a straight nose, firm jutting chin and close-shaved jawline showing a slight shadow of dark beard growth. He would probably need to shave twice a day like Ray did, she thought reflectively. Her eyes were drawn to his lips again and she quivered inside. Unbidden came the wonder of what it would feel like to have those lips move on hers.

At that precise moment he turned and caught her watching him, and Trista felt a rush of colour flood her face. Her heart was fluttering like a trapped bird and, embarrassed, she dropped her gaze from his. Then the heel of her shoe caught on the edge of a lifted plank and she felt herself falling.

Dylan's hands reached out and caught hold of her, steadying her, and didn't immediately set her free. Her eyes flashed upwards to meet his and it seemed as though the scene about them faded into the distance. The only area in focus was the small section that surrounded them. Even the sounds faded, the slap-slap of the water on the piles, the occasional voice, the cry of the gulls. All Trista could hear was the excited thudding of her heartbeats as they rose to deafen her.

Her hand went shakily of its own accord to rest against his chest, the slightly rough texture of his jacket searing her fingertips. The pressure of his fingers on her arms tightened as though he would draw her closer to the solidness of his hard body.

And how she wanted that, wanted to feel every last contour of him! Her body swayed towards him as though she had no control over its actions and her breath caught somewhere in her chest. For those few seconds she *had* lost all control, and that was a first for her. She'd never had that happen to her. It had been no great hardship for her to extricate herself from any physical contact with the few men who had come close to her. But this man . . .

A wave of revulsion rose like bile and she pushed away from him, letting the stiff breeze race between them. How could she have allowed him to come so close? What was she thinking of? This man of all men!

She could feel his eyes on her still. 'Thank you,' she said coolly, and began to walk on, unconsciously quickening her pace.

'Hey, what's the hurry? Those shoes aren't designed for this type of surface,' he ran his eyes downwards over her stocking-clad legs. 'You don't want to sprain your ankle.' He strode easily beside her, his long strides making a mockery of her haste.

She had felt his eyes slide down the long tanned length of her legs and she wished she'd worn a slacks-suit. The soft pleats of her lightweight skirt lifted in the breeze as she walked and his expression said he was appreciating the view.

The *Blue Dancer* stood out like a sore thumb in a group of three moored fishing boats. They passed Ray's boat, the *Shelly Star*, and Dylan's sharp eyes went from it to the *Avondale* tied beside it before his gaze fell on his inheritance.

At seventy-two feet in length with a twenty-three-foot beam, both capable of carrying nearly a hundred tonnes of fish below under refrigeration, the *Blue Dancer* was almost indentical to Ray's boat. But size and capacity were where the similarity ended.

The *Shelly Star* shone like a new pin, its paintwork fresh and decks clean and tidy. The Ashby boat used to be painted in smart blue and white, but now it looked a wreck of its former self. Paint peeled from its sides and dark trails of rust marred just about every part of it. The deck was unwashed and the bait tanks were obviously empty. It looked what it was, neglected and forlorn.

Trista watched a tightness take hold of the man beside her and a muscle jumped in the strong squareness of his jaw. There was a tense stillness in his stance. He was angry, and she admitted he had a right to be. No skipper worth his salt would allow a fine boat to deteriorate the way the *Blue Dancer* had.

'Who's been in charge?' he asked her, his eyes not leaving the boat.

'Gus Dean,' she replied softly, and he frowned. 'I can't say I know the name.'

'He's not from around here. I think he came over from Eden.' She paused. 'He should be on board.'

As if on cue a large lumbering man appeared on deck. He was dressed in tattered shorts slung below his protruding stomach and an even shabbier and dirty singlet, a growth of a few days' grey beard on his heavy face. He spared them an uninterested glance before turning away, his bare feet kicking with indifference at an untidy coil of rope as he raised a can of West End to his lips and drank thirstily.

'Mr Dean.' Trista's hand shaded her eyes against the glare off the water and she wished she'd thought to bring her sunglasses.

The man totally ignored her call and Dylan spoke with quiet authority. 'Dean!'

His tone brought the man around to face them.

'Yeah? Who wants him?' the gravelly voice replied reluctantly, the man's expression sullen.

Surefootedly Dylan sprang down on to the deck and turned to help Trista. His hand holding hers was firm and safe and she knew that same reluctance to have the pressure of his fingers release hers. She forced herself to step away from him. Space was what she needed, not this tense, charged proximity.

'Look, who said you could come aboard my boat?' The man was waving his can about belligerently. 'No one comes aboard my boat without my permission, see, so you can get off right now before I put you off!'

'I don't think you'd really want to try that, Dean,' Dylan said quietly, his voice honed steel for all its softness. 'Not if you know what's good for you.'

The older man weighed Dylan up and his eyes shifted nervously. 'What right have you got comin' on to my boat threatenin' me?' He had taken a step to the side, putting the safety of the bait tank between Dylan and himself.

'Your boat, Dean?' Dylan raised a mocking dark brow.

Gus Dean shifted uneasily again and his eyes swung to Trista.

'Who is this bloke, Miss Vaughan? He want to buy it? Did Hardie send you down here?'

'Yes, he did, but it's nothing to do with the sale of the *Blue Dancer*. This is the owner, Dylan Ashby,' said Trista, unable to suppress her satisfaction. Gus Dean was responsible for the deplorable state of the boat and she was pleased to see him taken aback.

'Ashby?' The man's head snapped back to Dylan. 'Ashby? You old Bill's son?'

Dylan inclined his head and with some reluctance Gus Dean stepped closer, wiping his hand down the side of his shorts before he held it out to the younger man.

'Pleased to meet you. Sorry I was a bit shirty. Can't be too careful about who comes on board, can you?'

'No, you can't at that,' Dylan agreed drily, his gaze running over the boat.

Gus Dean watched him warily. 'She needs a bit of work here and there, but old Bill wasn't interested in fixin' her up,' he shrugged. 'Nothin' a coat of paint won't fix. I could get the boys right on to it, if you give the word.'

Dylan strode across to lean on the hatchway, peering inside. Straightening, he dusted his hands together.

'That won't be necessary right now. One more day won't make much difference.' He regarded the other man levelly. 'We need to talk, Dean. I'll be back later this afternoon and I'd appreciate it if you could be here. Ready, Trista?' He turned to help her back on to the jetty, not waiting for any comment from Gus Dean. This time his hands almost spanned Trista's waist as he propelled her easily upwards.

'Say three o'clock, Dean,' he said to the other man, and taking Trista's arm he started them back towards the car, not giving the other man a glance.

His face was grim and Trista had to hurry to keep up with him. Halfway along he must have realised he was walking too fast for her, for he slowed his pace, his hands going into the pockets of his slacks.

'How long has that been going on?' he asked. 'Don't tell me, let me guess. From the financial reports I'd say the last three seasons. Right?'

'I guess so. That's when your father decided not to take the boat out himself and hired Gus,' she said.

Dylan made no comment on that and they strolled on in silence. Lost in her thoughts, very conflicting thoughts at that, Trista almost ran into Ray before she caught sight of him. That he had seen her, had stopped dead watching their approach, his face a mixture of incredulity and anger she recognised in the few seconds it took her to read his expression. Ray's eyes went from his sister to the man who had stopped by her side.

A genuine smile broke over Dylan's face as he reached out to clasp Ray's shoulder. 'Ray! I'd have known you anywhere,' he greeted him. 'How are you?'

'I'm fine, just fine,' Ray replied after a moment, and at his tone Dylan's smile became slightly wary.

'Well, what are you doing with yourself these days? I haven't had time to ask Trista yet,' he half turned to Trista and her eyes fell. 'Still fishing with the *Shelly Star*?'

Ray's gaze went back to his sister and Trista swallowed guiltily. She felt as though being seen with Dylan Ashby made her a traitor somehow in her brother's eyes.

'Ray, I . . .' She swallowed again. 'Trent had an appointment so he—well, he asked me to introduce Dy—Mr Ashby to Gus Dean.' Although she knew Dylan was watching her her eyes were unconsciously pleading with her brother.

Ray sighed faintly and patted her on the arm before turning back to the man beside her.

'Did Hardie mention I was interested in buying the *Blue Dancer*?' Ray faced Dylan squarely, his tone businesslike, although his expression was decidedly derogatory.

Dylan folded his arms and regarded Ray

through narrowed eyes. 'He mentioned a buyer, but not that it was you.'

'Your father had all but decided to sell,' Ray told him as the two men confronted each other. 'Is the boat still on the market?'

'It might be,' Dylan replied carefully. 'I haven't had much time to give it any thought.'

Ray's jaw tightened and he eyed Dylan stormily. 'When did you arrive back?'

'This morning,' Dylan told him, and Trista gasped in disbelief at his lie.

His eyes caught hers and he smiled. 'I passed through last Thursday on the way to visit my aunt and uncle in Wangary. I drove back here this morning,' he explained.

Ray nodded. 'If you do decide to sell the boat I'd appreciate it if you'd give me first refusal.' Ray raised his chin, meeting Dylan's gaze levelly, and Trista knew by the tightness around her brother's mouth just what it had cost Ray to ask for that concession.

'Sure,' Dylan agreed easily.

'Right. Well, I have to be going.' Ray moved around them. 'See you tonight, Tris.' And he was gone, striding up the jetty towards his boat.

Dylan watched Ray's retreating back, his expression closed, and as his eyes turned back to Trista she wondered if she had imagined a certain bleakness momentarily clouding their smooth dark brown depths.

'How about lunch?' he asked when they were re-seated in his car.

Trista's mouth went completely dry. 'Oh no. No, thank you. I have to get back.'

Dylan lifted the cuff of his jacket and glanced

at his watch. 'Even the most conscientious secretary deserves a lunch break at midday,' he smiled.

'I don't usually have a meal in the middle of the day.'

'You mean you don't eat at all at lunchtime?'

'No, not exactly. I'm just not used to a big meal. I have a salad roll or fruit, something like that.'

'Right, then that's what we'll have.' He reached out and flicked on the ignition and the car burbled to life. 'Where do they make the best ham and salad rolls these days?' he asked as he swung the car easily off in the direction of Tasman Terrace.

'But I have to get back to the office.' Trista tried again, without a lot of conviction, she admitted, as that traitorous part of her surged to the fore, wanting desperately to go with him.

'Nonsense! The answering service is on duty. It never sleeps,' he grinned, and any further objection she would have made died a sudden death as she smiled automatically back at him.

'Go straight ahead here,' she guided him softly.

'Where are we going?' Trista asked, their lunch sitting safely on her lap.

'Leave it to me. This is one place I haven't begun to forget,' Dylan laughed softly, and turned up the Flinders Highway and headed for Winters Hill. In no time he had stopped the car at the lookout and the rolling hillside slid downwards to the bay and the township.

'I've always loved this view,' he said, a quiet satisfied affection in his tone.

And it was beautiful. It was like looking down on a miniature tableau. To the left Boston Island guarded the bay, from this height a blue-tinged mirror dotted here and there with tiny boats; and there were the three piers, the silos, the matchbox-sized houses in neat rows between dark green trees. The coastline to the right wove into Proper Bay around the outcrop of the peninsular, an untouched wilderness of low scrub that was the Lincoln National Park, and disappeared towards Cape Catastrophe some forty kilometres away as the crow flies.

On a clear day, as this one was, you could pick out the white column of the Matthew Flinders Monument on Stamford Hill and the vague haze of a number of small islands past that in the deep blue Southern Ocean.

Dylan pointed out a couple of the islands, remembering most of their names. 'On an exceptionally clear day you can see Wedge Island with its precipitous eight-hundred-foot cliffs, can't you?'

Trista nodded as he sat back with a sigh.

'I can understand the Scottish soldier and his "not the hills of home",' he said softly, and they sat companionably finishing their lunch in silence.

'That's an odd sort of ship hove off Shelly Beach. Looks like a floating high-rise motel complex.' Dylan pointed out over the bay.

'It does, doesn't it? More especially at night when it's all lit up.' Trista sat forward in her seat. 'It's virtually a sea-going stockyard for livestock. There was some controversy about it in the beginning from the abattoir workers because meat is usually killed here and exported frozen.

However, some countries, mainly in the Middle East, stipulate live animals, so that's how they're transported. Makes it look top-heavy with all those tiers above the waterline, doesn't it?'

Dylan nodded. 'What's its carrying capacity?'

'About a hundred thousand head, I think.' Trista wrinkled her nose. 'When the boat's loading, sheep are brought here from all corners of the peninsular and the town seems to be overrun with bleating animals.'

'I can imagine,' he laughed, then he collected their food wrappers and empty cans together and climbed from the car to deposit them in the rubbish bin.

Trista got out of the car herself and stood by the small stone retaining wall gazing reflectively at the view. But she was barely registering it. Her mind was on Dylan Ashby and she was fighting herself. Her head told her to keep him in the worst perspective, but her body didn't seem to be listening. She was attuned to his presence. Even now her nerves were tingling as they sensed his long striding approach, were clamouring loudly as he stopped beside her, mere centimetres away from her.

'This used to be a popular night spot, I also seem to remember.' Dylan spoke. 'A parking spot, we used to call it, and sometimes it could get very congested up here,' he laughed quietly, the wind catching the sound and tossing it over her skin, making her nerve ends jump to attention. 'Ray and I used to bring our girl-friends up in your father's old sedan when Ray could talk him into letting us drive it. If you had a car you were in great demand with the ladies.'

'I'm sure you're underestimating yourself,' Trista remarked drily.

'Do you think so, Trista?' he asked with a softly teasing laugh that reduced her knees to water.

'Well, I'm only making a guess. I was, after all, only a baby myself at the time.'

'Ouch! That barb went home.' He laughed outright, belying his words, and slung an arm about her shoulders.

Trista stiffened, and he couldn't have helped feeling it, although he didn't remove his arm.

'You were about the cutest baby I ever saw, Tris, all blonde curls and big wide eyes.'

She pulled away from him then and turned back to the car, but his hand on her arm stayed her retreat.

'Tris, I was only teasing you!'

'Well, I'd rather you didn't,' she told him coldly, her eyes not meeting his.

Dylan's fingers lifted her chin until she was looking straight at him. 'You also used to have a sense of humour,' he said quietly. 'What happened to that?'

'Perhaps I left it back there,' she told him.

His eyes seemed to bore down deep inside her and she was afraid of what he might see.

Her hand brushed his fingers from her chin. 'And I don't care to be pawed about.' She went to move away, but his fingers clasped her forearms like vices and, startled, she looked up to see a very real anger had turned his brown eyes to inky black.

'I'd say you left your manners back there, too, Trista,' he bit out. 'From where I stood I was hardly pawing you.' His jaw tightened. 'I'm beginning to think you're long overdue for a good paddle on that nice little backside of yours. And I'm quite capable of giving it to you.'

'You wouldn't dare!' Trista tried to break his hold, but he held her fast.

'Never dare me, Trista. That's just asking for trouble.' His anger had cooled a little, but he still didn't let her go. His gaze fell to her mouth as she caught her breath, her white teeth catching her full bottom lip as her heartbeats stumbled agitatedly in her breast.

At that moment her eyes, her whole nervous system recorded the change in the timbre of his hold. She pushed her hands against his chest as she recognised the subtle variation from pure anger to an aggressive sexuality. The attraction between them that had been chipping away at the surface from below had now broken out, surged into the already charged atmosphere between them and caught Trista in its spell.

Wordlessly, immobile, she watched his lips as they descended without haste. It was as though he had hypnotised her, and her fingers curled into the front of his shirt beneath his open jacket. She had to do something, she told herself screamingly, she had to stop him before he kissed her, because if he did kiss her it would be too late.

CHAPTER FOUR

'No!' The word was wrenched huskily from her, a broken whisper made a mockery by the tumbling breeze.

He hovered over her, each passing second a millenium, and she began to move her head from side to side.

'No, Dylan!'

His eyes taunted, were alight with laughter that barely cloaked the passion that smouldered in their dark depths.

'There are more ways than one to teach a lesson that needs to be learned, Tris, much more enjoyable means of punishment.'

His lips found hers then and from that moment, when his mouth closed on hers, she was lost in a whirling kaleidoscope of sensations she couldn't have imagined existed. She made no effort now to escape. She was incapable of backing away. Her whole body stepped out to meet him, locked with his, his lips potently persuasive probing the softness of her pliant mouth, her body achingly arched to fit each aroused contour of his.

And their soul-searching kisses, drugging kisses, were not enough. The closeness of their merging bodies was not enough. Dylan's lips surrendered her mouth, slid over her jaw to the softness of her throat, tantalised the sensitivity of her earlobe and when she moaned huskily she heard him catch his breath.

'God, Trista, this is crazy,' he murmured as his fingertips teased her backbone, propelling her impossibly closer to his muscular thighs. 'Crazy. Just crazy,' he repeated, his tone sending shivers within her.

Trista's fingers wound themselves into the darkness of his hair luxuriating in its clean crispness. Her breasts, crushed against his chest, swelled, throbbed, and when his hand slid around her ribcage to cup one full globe his fingers sought and found with ease her erect nipple.

A wave of pure desire washed over her, rose to engulf her entire body and she sagged against him, her legs refusing to hold her. Dylan braced himself back against the car, holding her tightly to him, his breathing raw and ragged as his lips claimed hers again.

A small part of her recognised that they were both far more aroused than they should have allowed themselves to be, but Trista was powerless to make the move to stop Dylan's urgent kisses, his control-destroying caresses. And he was as aroused as she was. Standing in the tight circle of his arms, one long tensed leg on either side of her, Trista was in no doubt about that. His heightened excitement fanned the flame of desire that burned within her and for the first time in her life she knew she was fast approaching the point of no return.

It was the wolf-whistle that penetrated her aroused euphoria, and her fingers stilled in the act of unbuttoning his shirt, her face flooding with colour as a car drove past them, around the circular road and then disappeared down the hill with a roar.

Trista could have died of mortification. How long had the other carload of people been there? She had been so carried away by Dylan's lovemaking she hadn't been aware of the sound of the car's approach. And neither apparently had Dylan.

He went to draw her back into his arms, but she stepped away from him, her hands fumbling in jerky movements as she began to shove her blouse back into the waistband of her skirt.

The corners of Dylan's mouth lifted derisively. 'Now that's what I call bad timing,' he said ruefully as his eyes continued to drink in the still agitated rise and fall of her breasts. His ardent gaze only made her more clumsy as, embarrassed, she could feel her nipples thrust against the thin material of her blouse.

'Please don't,' she got out painfully.

'Please don't look at you?' He raised one dark eyebrow. 'That's a tall order, I'm afraid,' he said, his voice low and still vibrating with a deep sensuousness. He moved away from the car in one fluid movement, his own fingers sure as he rebuttoned his shirt.

'I think we should be getting back.' Her voice was still tight, unlike her own, and she was totally incapable of preventing her eyes from running over him.

His hair was still slightly disturbed where her fingers had slid excitedly through its thickness. And yet the rise and fall of his chest implied he was not as calm and unruffled as his sure movements indicated. Undoing his belt, he tucked in his shirt and Trista's face flamed as her gaze slid downwards over his taut thighs.

She closed her eyes, cringing inwardly. If they hadn't been interrupted how far would she have allowed that embrace to go? That was ludicrous. She had had absolutely no control over the situation at all and she knew it.

'Pity,' he murmured as he stepped closer again and one strong hand reached up to tuck a strand of wind-tossed hair back behind her ear, his fingertips lingering on the sensitive curve of her neck.

A tingle of awareness rose again and her eyelids flickered as she fought to stop herself from turning to kiss his palm as it cupped the side of her face.

'Don't do that! Anyone could come along and see us. That other car did. It could be all over town by this evening.' Her words were tormented. 'I'd hate that,' she finished vehemently, her body stiffening at the thought of the gossip, the snide comments.

'Who cares?' Dylan asked levelly.

'I do. I care!' Her anger drew a furrow between her brows.

Dylan's eyes moved over her face. 'It matters that much to you?' he asked after a pause.

'Of course it matters!'

'Why?'

'You can ask that?' Her throat constricted painfully.

'I'd say it was a reasonable question,' he stated evenly. 'And it might be as well if you explain it to me.'

'I wouldn't have said it needed an explanation.'

Dylan's dark eyes regarded her piercingly. 'And I wouldn't have asked if I didn't think one was necessary,' he said, a tinge of exasperation in his tone. 'Look, Trista,' he leant back against the car and folded his arms, 'you're over twenty-one and presumably unattached . . .'

'How could you know that?' she broke in on him.

His gaze settled on her lips again as his eyelids fell to shutter the expression in those dark eyes. 'Are you unattached?' he asked quietly.

Trista turned away, wishing she had the nerve to tell a blatant lie and finish all this once and for all. Maybe if she mentioned Trent's name . . .

'You're unattached,' Dylan said flatly, 'and so am I. I wanted to kiss you, I've wanted to do it since I saw you down by the shore. And you wanted me to kiss you.'

'I did not!' Trista coloured.

He gave a short disbelieving laugh. 'That's not how I read it.'

'Then you read it wrongly,' she snapped, trying to believe her denial herself.

'Did I? Oh, no, Trista, I don't somehow think so. I know the signs.' His smile didn't touch his eyes.

'I don't doubt you know the signs, as you put it, you've had enough practice. But this time you made a mistake. Now I'd like to go back to work.' She lifted her chin.

'So I've had enough practice, have I? What gives you that idea, Tris? I'm afraid I can't admit to having more than my humble share of—er—practice.' A thread of amusement was lurking in his eyes now. 'What man wouldn't admit to it?'

'You're despicable!' Trista seethed.

'Good grief, girl, do you expect me to profess

to be a virgin?' A frown of annoyance wiped away the amusement and he straightened, his hands aggressively on his narrow hips.

'You're hardly that.' A tide of embarrassed colour flooded her face.

'Thank you.' Dylan inclined his head mockingly. 'Dare I take that as a vote of confidence in my technique?' He made a sound of exasperation. 'Trista, I can't see why you're making such an issue of it. I kissed you, you kissed me. We kissed——'

Trista opened her mouth to butt in, but he held up one hand to silence her.

'We kissed each other,' he continued. 'And someone saw us. Is that so calamitous?'

'It is to me. I don't want to be seen with you, Dylan Ashby,' she said heatedly.

'With me particularly or with anyone?'

'With anyone, particularly you!'

He was silent, his eyes assessing her expression, and she had the impression again that he was searching down into her very soul.

'I haven't been home for thirteen years. What could you possibly have against me in particular?' he asked quietly.

'You must be joking!' Trista exclaimed.

'That's the last thing I'd be doing.' He frowned. 'Is it the *Blue Dancer*?'

'The *Blue Dancer*?' Trista's eyes widened in surprise before her anger revived. 'I don't give a damn about the boat!' Her voice rose a little shrilly.

'Then if it's not the boat what the devil is it?'

'I just don't believe you!' she spluttered and made herself take a steadying breath. 'All right,

Mr Dylan Ashby. You want to know, so I'll give it to you straight. I don't fancy having my name bandied about with yours, not after the way you left Lincoln in the first place!'

His mouth was set in a hard line, his eyes stormily cold. 'How the hell could my reasons for leaving Port Lincoln have anything to do with you? What would you know about it?'

'What would——? The whole town knows why you left Port Lincoln, that's how I know!' she raged at him.

'And tell me, why should the town be half interested in me or something that happened years ago? The whole thing was boiling to happen anyway and had been for long enough,' he finished with a twist of his lips.

'Boiling to—— My God, you're disgusting! How can you stand there so barefacedly when you broke up a family?' she appealed to him.

Dylan's lips thinned and he drew a sharp breath. 'It wouldn't have broken up if it hadn't been cracked, and the split had been there for as long as I can remember.'

Trista could only stand and stare at him, her anger rendering her speechless. He showed no regret for what he'd done. And no remorse.

'And it seems to me that I can go back further than you can,' he continued, his voice softer now, controlled. 'You could only have been a child at the time, six or seven, so someone had to tell you the tale. It must have come second-hand.'

'I was eight years old and I remember it vividly. No one had to tell me anything. Not one thing,' she bit out. 'Not that it stopped them,' she added with bitterness.

Dylan's long dark lashes shielded the expression in his eyes as they faced each other, the anger heavy in the air about them, and although Trista felt that anger spit from her like tongues of flame it wasn't all-consuming. Her awareness of him burned with it, a shaft of physical attraction that still skipped across the space between them, the anger and awareness warring inside her, filling her with an unnerving confusion.

What kind of person was she? This man had virtually ruined their lives, hers and Ray's, their father's, and she'd allowed him to kiss her, to caress her far more intimately than any other man had done. She shrank within herself with self-disgust.

Well, what's done is done, she told herself forcefully, and she must just see it didn't happen again. Ever. Her senses shivered, remembering. If only—— What good would that do? she admonished herself, and took a steadying breath.

'I'd like to go back to the office,' she repeated calmly.

For a long moment Dylan didn't move. His eyes watched her and their expression was inscrutable, his face set, his lips thin. Slowly he turned and without a word he opened the passenger side door of the car and moved back for her to climb inside.

Those few steps towards him, past his tall solidness, within a hand's touch of him, took all Trista's gathered courage, and she subsided into the luxurious upholstery of the seat feeling tense as a coiled spring.

And when he joined her it was impossibly worse. She kept her eyes to the front, but that didn't mean she was unaware of him, of every slight movement he made—the reaching out of his tanned hand to switch on the ignition, the shifting of his feet on brake and clutch, his hand now on the gear lever. And then they moved off, back towards the township laid out below them.

Out of the corner of her eye she watched the smooth material of his trousers stretched over the tautness of his thighs and her body began to glow with a fiery warmth. She wanted to feel his body against hers again and she had to use all her willpower to stop herself from reaching across to touch him.

What was happening to her? She'd never had such thoughts, never wanted to touch a man the way she yearned to run her hands over this man. And he wasn't just any man. He was Dylan Ashby. Dylan Ashby, she reminded herself angrily, repeating the name over and over. Dylan Ashby. Remember that and remember what he did.

If there was any anger left in him it didn't show in his driving. He turned the car evenly around corners until they were back at Trista's office and he drew the car smoothly to a stop.

Trista went to open the door, but his hand was on the catch before she could take hold of it, his body reaching across, achingly close to hers. She shrank back into the upholstery and his mouth tightened as his eyes skimmed her face.

'Trista, I'm not a fisherman—I never have been. My family knew that. As a sport, a relaxation, I enjoy it—growing up in a fishing town I couldn't help that. But as a profession it's always left me cold. If that damns me in your eyes then so be it.' He swung open the door and sat back behind the wheel. 'Tell Trent I'll give him a call in a few days,' he said flatly, and his fingers tapped impatiently on the steering wheel as he waited for her to climb out on to the pavement.

And Trista had no desire to prolong their interlude. She all but fell out of the car, closing the door behind her, walking quickly across to the entrance, not looking back, not stopping until the door of the office was closed firmly behind her.

'There, Trista?' Ray's head appeared around the open door of her flat.

'Hi! Come on in.' Trista steeled herself knowing what, or in this case, who, Ray wanted to discuss. She had been expecting him to come downstairs since she arrived home over an hour ago. 'Did you get the part for the engine?'

'What? Oh, the engine. Yes. It wasn't a big job. We finished earlier this afternoon.' Ray stood beside the old lead glass-fronted dresser that had belonged to their grandmother. 'You gave me a bit of a shock today,' he said without preamble. 'I wasn't expecting to see you at the wharf, and I sure as hell didn't expect to see you with Dylan Ashby.'

'I know that. You don't think I wanted to be with him, do you?' Trista's tone sounded sharp and snappy in her ears and she sighed as she hung her damp tea-towel over the rack by the sink. 'I . . . Trent coudn't get away this morning, so he asked me to take Dy . . . him down to the *Blue Dancer*. I couldn't get out of it.'

Ray stood quietly watching her for a moment and then nodded. 'I guessed it was something like that. Obviously Trent hasn't heard the juicy details or he wouldn't have asked you to do it.' He crossed the small kitchen and pulled out a chair, turning it around so that he could sit astride it, resting his arms along the back. 'What kind of reaction did he have when he saw the boat?'

Trista sat down at the table opposite her brother. 'What do you think? He doesn't give much away, but I imagine you could safely say he wasn't happy about the *Blue Dancer* or Gus Dean.' She shuddered. 'Obnoxious man! How old Mr Ashby could have hired a man like that as the skipper of his boat I'll never understand. Ugh!'

'Well, obnoxious or not, Gus got the boot,' Ray said with not a little pleasure.

'The boot? You mean Dylan fired him? Already?' Trista asked incredulously.

'This afternoon.' Ray gave a crooked smile. 'Can't say anyone will blame him for that. He fired the entire crew without blinking an eye, no questions asked, so I heard.'

A slight frown sat on Trista's brow. 'Do you think he means to work the *Blue Dancer* himself now?'

'Who knows?' Ray shrugged. 'Maybe he'll just hire another crew. The last lot were a lazy mob of no-hopers, that's for sure, so he couldn't do worse. Anyway, the boat's around at the slip, out of the water, about to undergo what sounds like a major overhaul.'

'Who told you all this?'

Ray shrugged again. 'Word gets around—you know how it is. But the boat's out of the water for sure. I went around and checked that myself, and I have to say it's not in as bad a shape as I thought it was.'

'Oh, Ray! If only Mr Ashby had sold it to you before he died,' Trista began sympathetically.

'What the heck! Then I'd be the one footing the bill instead of Dylan Ashby. And it won't be cheap.' Ray sighed. 'I've managed with one boat up till now, so I don't see why I can't keep on managing with just the *Shelly Star*. One thing's for sure, I won't be able to afford the new price Dylan Ashby will most certainly put on the *Blue Dancer*.' He rubbed his chin reflectively. 'I just wish for all our sakes that that bastard hadn't come back. I don't see why he didn't just sell out for what he could get without putting in an appearance. That would have been more in keeping with his form.'

Trista made no comment and her fingers twisted together in her lap. How she wished that too, wished she'd never met Dylan Ashby, never gone with him to Winters Hill, never been so foolish as to let him touch her, kiss her, caress her the way he had. She cringed with self-disgust again, hating herself for being so weak. It would be a long time before she would be able to trust herself not to act so foolishly.

'It must have been tough on you, Tris,' Ray broke in on her self-berating. 'I mean, you had to take him down there, talk to him.'

A quick nod was all she could manage and a guilty flush washed her cheeks.

'Did he say anything?' Ray asked quietly, a little stiffly.

'What . . . What about?' Trista tried to swallow the choking lump in her throat as she played for time.

'About our mother.' Ray's voice held that same bitter note.

'No, he didn't mention her.' Trista frowned. 'Now I come to think about it, it was pretty strange. All he said was that he wasn't a fisherman and he seemed surprised that the whole town knew the reason he left. Surely he would have known people would talk?'

'Of course he would have known,' Ray said angrily. 'He'd lived in Lincoln all his life. We're a pretty isolated community compared with the sprawling cities. It's only natural everyone's interested in what everyone else is doing. Anyway, how often does a married woman run off with someone young enough to be her son? It sure doesn't happen every day around here.'

'He didn't seem guilty or sorry,' said Trista, half to herself, and a tiny spark of hope lit a glow inside her, surprising her with its importance. 'Ray, you don't think there was any mistake about it, do you? I mean, about Dylan Ashby being involved.' She was unaware of the soft appeal in her eyes, and her brother was taken aback.

It crossed his mind as he saw the expression she couldn't conceal that Dylan Ashby was good-looking charming—he always had been. And he'd always had his choice of girls, even as a teenager. With something of a shock Ray realised his baby sister was hardly a child any longer. She was an attractive young woman. And Dylan Ashby was still as good looking as he'd ever been.

But *Trista?* Ray's anger stirred again and he wanted to reach out for Dylan Ashby with his bare hands and . . . He drew himself together.

'What sort of mistake?' he asked as evenly as he could.

'Maybe he didn't—well, go off with our mother.' There, it was out. She'd said it. And her eyes watched her brother for his reaction. 'Did our mother . . . did she actually say she was leaving with Dylan Ashby? You've never really told me any of the details.'

Ray stood up and prowled restlessly about the small kitchen, not saying anything for long moments, before turning back to her. 'Tris, I'm sorry, but there was no mistake.'

He sat down again as Trista's eyes fell to her hands again. 'She sent Dad a note,' he said flatly. 'From Adelaide. She was supposed to be going over there for a few days' shopping, but the next thing the letter arrived saying she wasn't coming back. She said she was in love with someone else, that they'd been in love for some time and rather than embarrass both families they were going away to make a new life together.' Ray's lips twisted. 'She asked our forgiveness and understanding, and that was it.'

'She didn't mention any name?' Trista asked.

'She didn't have to. Dylan often drove her about, gave her lifts into town.' Ray's eyes steadily met his sister's. 'Someone had already told Dad that she'd been seen in Dylan's car out at Sleaford and up on Winters Hill. Dad didn't believe it at the time.'

On Winters Hill. Trista's heart contracted with pain. How could he even think of taking her there when he'd been there before with her mother? God, he was despicable! And what was she, to have let him touch her the way he had?

'Tris!' Ray said her name worriedly as he watched her face pale. 'Are you okay?'

'Yes. Yes, I'm all right.' She dropped her eyes. 'So there's no mistake?'

'No, there's no mistake. It had to be him all right.' Ray looked as though he was about to say more but pushed himself to his feet. 'I guess I should get back to Joanne.' He stopped at the door and turned back to face her. 'I don't suppose Trent said anything about Dylan's plans for the boat, did he?'

Trista shook her head. She could sympathise with Ray over his impatience to have the issue of the *Blue Dancer* settled, but the tuna boat at that moment was the very least of her worries.

'That dress looks great, Trista,' Joanne remarked as Ray held open the door of his uncharacteristically clean sedan for his wife to climb inside. 'I'd say, Raymond Vaughan, that you were the luckiest man in Lincoln having Trista and me, the best-looking girls in town, to escort to this wedding.' She smiled teasingly at her husband.

'I'm overcome by the emotion of it all,' grinned Ray, then ran his finger irritatedly inside the collar of his shirt. 'Or maybe it's just this damn tight collar.'

'Charming!' laughed Joanne. 'If you got yourself dressed up a little more often you'd be more used to it.'

'I'll never get used to it. I feel like a Port Phillip penguin,' Ray pulled a face.

'You're not furry enough,' Trista smiled as she settled herself in the car. She had to admit she felt rather good in her new outfit. The pale green colour of the cool crêpe material suited her colouring, her lightish brown hair bleached fair on the ends from the time she spent in the sunshine, and the colour seemed to bring out the green flecks in her hazel eyes.

She could understand Ray's discomfort in his tailored suit, for it was quite hot and a little humid. The top of her dress left her shoulders and arms bare and the skirt was full enough to be quite cool on this hot day.

Trista wasn't much looking forward to the afternoon, but as she had known the groom, a friend of Ray's, since her childhood she felt she should attend the wedding even though she hadn't taken advantage of the 'and friend' on the invitation. At first she had considered asking Trent to attend as her partner, but that might have given him the wrong idea about her intentions.

So she was on her own as usual, she thought, grimacing at the small sigh that escaped before she could catch it back. She rarely indulged in such self-pity and she wasn't going to start now.

At least her lack of a partner wouldn't stir any gossiping tongues to wagging. Everyone was used to seeing her on her own. To have arrived with her boss, Trent Hardie, would have been asking for comment.

Ray turned the car into London Street and they crossed the railway bridge. The multi-coloured sails of a group of small yachts were heading out into the blue of the bay.

'I'm glad our wedding day wasn't as hot as this,' remarked Joanne, fanning herself with her clutch purse. 'My dress would have had me dehydrating!'

'If I remember rightly it blew like mad, didn't it?' Ray turned the corner and slid the car slowly into the kerb just past the church. 'Maybe the weather was forecasting stormy times ahead,' he laughed.

'I'll give you stormy times!' Joanne retaliated. 'You don't know when you're well off, that's your trouble.'

'Oh yes, I do.' He leaned over to give her a quick kiss on the cheek before climbing out of the car.

The little church was already over half full and they moved into a vacant pew a couple of rows from the back. There was a whispered murmur of conversation and the rustle of the paper sheets showing the order of the service which the ushers were handing out.

'Looks like we'll be having a full house,' commented Ray softly, and Joanne admonished him with her eyes.

At that moment the groom and his best man entered from a side door to take their places at the front of the church and a number of ladies craned their necks towards the door for the first glimpse of the bride. About to glance around herself, Trista noticed an elderly matron in a seat on the opposite side of the aisle nudge the woman beside her and both pairs of eyes widened with surprise.

Before she could begin to wonder what had caused the stir, for now a number of other people were whispering excitedly, a figure moved down the aisle to their pew and slipped into the empty seat beside her. And that figure was drawing more attention than the bride as she stood waiting for her cue to begin her walk down the aisle.

CHAPTER FIVE

IN those few seconds Trista was aware of great height and breadth of shoulder clad in a dark brown suit, of dark hair, a rugged square jaw, deep black eyes and the heady faint tang of a clean-smelling aftershave that was redolent of the sunlit sea.

She could have shrivelled up and died. How dared he? Of all the seats in the church why did he have to pick a place beside her? Surely he couldn't be so naïve as to imagine it would go unnoticed. Or had he done it on purpose? Was he making some coldly diverting point of his own?

Even now the strong trouser-clad leg was resting mere millimetres from hers and as he undid the button on his suit coat the smoothness of the expensive material of his sleeve brushed her bare arm. She could have cried out at the force of the wave of awareness that washed over her. Yet she should be outraged. She should stand up, change her seat, let him and everyone in the congregation know here and now she had no wish to be near him, no desire—No desire.

What she really wanted to do, if she was totally honest with herself, was to rest her hand on the tautness of his thigh, spread her fingers out against the background of the smooth dark material stretched tightly over the strength of those hard muscles.

Trista was absolutely horrified at her thoughts.

Here they sat in church and she—— Tiny beads of perspiration broke out on her brow, and feeling slightly sick, she fumbled shakily in her bag for her handkerchief, gently daubing at her clammy skin.

Unconsciously she slid a little closer to Joanne who moved along towards Ray. He shuffled down the pew, looking around to see why his wife had moved. Trista watched her brother's face change expression as his eyes met Dylan Ashby's across the two girls. Ray's lips tightened and he sat back folding his arms with slow constraint.

How Ray's so obvious displeasure affected Dylan Ashby Trista had no way of knowing because she couldn't bring herself to look at him.

The organist began the traditional strains of 'Here Comes the Bride' and the congregation climbed to its feet. What an attractive picture the bride made, how embarrassingly proud the father of the bride looked beside her or what the minister said Trista couldn't have told. She stood stiffly beside that tall dark figure oblivious of anything and anyone else around her.

'May I?' His voice murmured quietly for her ears only and his tanned hand reached out to take the printed order of service sheet, opening it to the words of the hymn the organist had begun to play.

O Perfect Love. His singing voice was as throbbingly deep, as blatantly sensual as his speaking voice and Trista's own vocal chords froze, totally incapable of rendering a note.

For the remainder of the ceremony, a quite reasonably short service which seemed to Trista to be drawn out for interminable hours, her nerves were stretched to screaming pitch. The well-known hymn of love flowed about her, but she didn't consciously hear it, for her heart was racing to a far different tune. It throbbed her awareness, sensitive to each movement he made, however slight.

Eventually it was over, the bride moving down the aisle on the arm of her new husband, followed by the bridesmaid and best man and both sets of parents. Then the rest of the relatives and friends began to file out after them. Dylan stood waiting patiently and out of the corner of her eye Trista saw him smile greetings to a number of acquaintances who had no trouble recognising him. If their eyes slid over to Trista she wasn't aware of it, for she found she couldn't bear to look at them.

Dylan stepped into the aisle, but instead of moving off he stood back for Trista to precede him, which she was forced to do or else she would have held everyone up. He walked beside her, seemingly oblivious of Ray's cold stare and the heavy air of his frowning disapproval that hung thickly about them.

The bright sunlight hit Trista's eyes as she stepped on trembling legs out of the church and she groped for the steadiness of the rail on the stairs. But a strong arm was there before her fingers encountered the railing.

'Mind the step,' he said, and she was guided solicitously down into the milling group of guests.

'Thank you,' Trista mumbled, feeling a flush of red wash her face as she met the sharp eyes of Gay Richards, one of the girls she had overheard talking in the boutique.

Gay's eyes widened and then her lips tightened as she recognised Dylan at Trista's side, and to Trista's horror she watched the other girl move towards them.

'Hello, Trista,' Gay said cursorily before she turned to the man beside Trista. 'Well, well, I thought I was seeing things!' she smiled now, her strident voice carrying, attracting the attention of a number of people in their vicinity. 'Dylan Ashby, isn't it?' her smile widened as she held out her hand. 'I'm Gay Richards, Wayne's sister.'

Dylan smiled back and took the offered hand. 'Wayne's sister? Yes, I remember you,' he said silkily. 'How are you?'

'I'm fine, just fine. When did you arrive back home?' she asked.

Trista was sure the other girl had actually fluttered her eyelashes at him and she felt a spurt of anger rise in her, overriding her embarrassment. Looking up at Dylan as he stood beside her with the sunshine gleaming on his dark head, she could understand the slightly dazed expression on Gay's face. He was by far the most attractive man she'd ever seen, and her own nerve ends were clamouring inside her at his nearness.

'I arrived back last week,' Dylan was telling Gay. 'And I seem to have brought some of Queensland's hot weather with me.'

'Oh, you've been in Queensland?' Trista could almost see Gay treasuring that bit of information to relate later. 'And what have you been doing with yourself up North?'

'As little as possible,' Dylan laughed, and Gay joined in heartily, the sound rasping Trista's nerves like scraping chalk on a blackboard.

'Don't we all?' Gay agreed. 'Are you coming to the reception?'

'Yes. I believe Tom's new in-laws have found me a spot at one of the tables, even though it was short notice.'

'That was kind of them,' simpered Gay. 'They're nice people. They came from Whyalla, I think, and they've been in Lincoln for about two years.'

Some of the guests were leaving for the reception now that the photographer had taken his shots of the bridal group and a rather innocuous-looking man walked up to them and asked Gay if she was ready to go.

'Yes, of course.' Gay was more than a little short with him. 'Well, I guess we'll see you at the reception.' She reluctantly moved off and Dylan turned back to Trista, his eyes going from her to Ray and Joanne as they stood with her.

'Do you need a lift to the reception?' he asked easily, his offer directed at the three of them.

'No, thank you. I have my car,' Ray replied dismissingly.

'Okay. See you later, then.' Dylan walked over towards the group clustered around the bride and groom.

Trista's eyes unconsciously followed his tall figure as he moved away from them. His dark suit fitted his broad shoulders like a second skin, emphasising the hard muscles beneath. He was now standing waiting his turn to offer his congratulations to Tom and Maree. Trista's gaze skimmed the group, noticing that Dylan's dark head seemed to stand out from everyone else's and he was the tallest man in the group.

Just then a fair-haired man and a petite dark-haired girl stepped across to stand to one side of Dylan, and Trista recognised Troy Aimes. Without a qualm she watched him turn to speak to the girl beside him. Somehow she would have expected Troy's presence at the wedding to have unnerved her, but the sight of him had no effect on her whatsoever, her whole nervous system seemed tuned to Dylan Ashby. She was a puppet and Dylan Ashby pulled the string.

'So that's Dylan Ashby,' said Joanne, unable to keep the tinge of admiration out of her voice. 'He's certainly a handsome devil.'

'Handsome? Like hell he is!' scowled Ray. 'He's all smooth talk, that's all he is. And he sure hasn't wasted any time insinuating himself back into the social scene. I don't know what Tom was about inviting him to the wedding. Humph! He probably invited himself.'

'Well, next time he comes over you'd better introduce us,' began Joanne, half teasingly.

'Introduce you to that . . . I wouldn't introduce him to water if he was dying of thirst!' He turned his frown on Trista as she stood unhappily beside them. 'What a nerve he's got, sitting next to you in the church. If he thinks he can start making something between you and him he's got another think coming!'

Trista flushed scarlet.

'Now, Ray, stop playing the heavy father figure with Trista.' Joanne put a soothing hand on her husband's arm. 'Trista's a big girl now and she can decide for herself who she wants to be friendly with.'

Ray spluttered, 'She doesn't want to be palsy with him!'

'Ray, keep your voice down. You'll be roaring like a bull in a minute,' Joanne said evenly.

'Maybe it was the only vacant seat,' Trista said placatingly.

'There were seats behind us.' Ray shrugged his shoulders uncomfortably in his suit. 'I'm not having him leching after you, Trista!'

'Ray, I didn't ask him to sit there,' Trista stated crisply, tired of the whole conversation, tired of Dylan Ashby.

'Of course she didn't, Ray, so calm down. Heaven help our poor baby if it's a girl, that's all I can say! Anyway, from the number of admiring glances Dylan Ashby's getting I'd say there'd be plenty of girls who wouldn't mind him sitting next to them. Trista may have to stand in line.'

A sharp pain seemed to wedge in Trista's chest at Joanne's lightly spoken words and she tried hard not to turn to follow the direction of Dylan Ashby. She didn't need to look at him to remember how good-looking he was. His face, each feature deeply etched, was printed indelibly in her mind's eye.

'Sounds like you might fancy him yourself,' growled Ray, and Joanne laughed, winking across at Trista.

'Nonsense! You know very well I only have eyes for you, darling,' she said sweetly, and added softly, 'mostly.'

Ray smiled reluctantly. 'I think I'm being got at again. Come on, he's left now. We can go and congratulate Tom and Maree.'

The wedding reception was being held in Tom's parents' garden. A large marquee stretched beneath the green leaves of the Chinese elm trees over rows of tables and chairs set out to seat about eighty guests. Tom's father was a keen gardener and his flowers added a bright variegation of colour to the setting.

The meal was to be a smörgasbörd style and two tables were already chock-a-block with delicious-smelling homestyle food. Tom's youngest brother had started filling beer glasses from the keg as the male contingent gathered around.

The afternoon sun lit the lovely old house, bringing out the soft tones of the quarried limestone blocks. The house had been in Tom's family for over a hundred years and the blocks from which it was built had been cut behind the town.

With Ray and Joanne, Trista approached the outdoor setting and one of Tom's young cousins ran to find their places at the tables for them.

'I think you're here, Ray,' called Tom's sister as she passed them carrying a tray of small dishes of peanuts and sweets to be placed on the tables.

'Thanks, Sue.' Ray pulled out a chair for Joanne and she sank thankfully on to it. 'What will you two have to drink?'

They both decided on lemonade and Ray strode off to get the soft drinks and a beer for himself.

'Are you on the opposite side, Tris?' Joanne asked as she glanced at the place card on the table beside her. 'We've got Gay Richards and her current escort on this side.'

Trista walked around the white clothed table. 'Yes. I'm on the end here next to . . .' Her voice faded away.

'Next to?' Joanne prompted.

'Oh, no! Ray'll blow his top!' she whispered. And Ray wasn't the only one who'd be disturbed by the seating arrangements. How was she going to sit out the entire reception?

'Ah! Found your seats all right, have you?' Mrs King, the bride's mother, bustled up to them. 'I hope you don't mind us putting Mr Ashby at your table, it was the only one with a spare seat and I believe he's a friend of your family as well as Tom's. Now, I must see that my husband has the wine in hand.' She hurried off, her portly figure slightly flustered.

'Oh no!' Joanne echoed Trista's words. 'We'd better find Ray and warn him. Can you see him anywhere, Tris?'

Trista turned towards the group of men by the keg, searching for Ray's dark head. At last she spotted him making his way towards them.

'Drinks for everyone.' He set the glasses down and began slipping out of his jacket. 'Thank heavens I can dispense with this. Official permission of the father of the bride.' He hung his coat over the back of his chair. 'I feel like I've been in a Turkish bath all afternoon!'

'Ray, there's something you should know,' Trista began softly, but before she could continue a deep voice spoke beside her.

'Hello again. Mrs King said I was seated with you.' Dylan picked up his card and set it down again, taking a sip of the cold amber beer he held in his other hand.

Ray's face froze and Joanne reached up to put her hand on his arm.

'Ray!' She waited until his gaze moved from Dylan to herself. 'You haven't introduced us,' she said quietly, and Trista saw the silent appeal she made to Ray not to create a scene.

'This is my wife, Joanne,' Ray said a trifle ungraciously, and Joanne offered her hand to the tall man beside Trista.

'Please excuse Ray. I think he forgets me if I don't remind him I'm here,' she smiled as she shook hands. 'And you're Dylan Ashby.' She slanted a rebuke at Ray.

'I am. How do you do? You seem far too nice to be tied up with Ray Vaughan. How did he manage to convince you to take him on?'

Trista only caught the edge of his smile and her knees wobbled weakly so she could understand her sister-in-law's bubbly smile as Dylan Ashby turned on his charm.

'I don't know. How did you manage it, love?' she smiled up at Ray.

'Swept you off your feet and didn't give you time to refuse.' Ray relaxed a little and put his hand on Joanne's shoulder.

'And this is your first baby?' Dylan asked, and Joanne nodded.

'Yes, our first. We've waited a long time for junior here.' Joanne patted the mound of her stomach.

'Dylan, are you at our table?' Gay's strident voice cut across their conversation. 'Oh, lovely! Rose—Bill—come and see who's back!' Gay drew a couple forward and Trista recognised the girl as Rose Eden, one of the other girls she'd heard talking to Gay in the boutique.

The couple were Ray's age and their eyes went from Ray and Trista to Dylan Ashby and they were clearly embarrassed. Trista wished she could sink into the ground and she knew the telltale colour was flooding her face again. And it was all Dylan Ashby's fault. Here she was standing like a stuffed dummy with the tongue-ties while he was charm itself, not a sign of any guilt for his past actions.

'You remember Dylan, don't you, Bill?' Gay was saying. 'He was at school with you and Ray and my brother, Wayne.'

'Yes, of course.' Bill held out his hand. 'Good to see you again, Dylan.' He smiled across at Ray and Joanne and Rose murmured hello to Trista.

Then they were all laughing and talking at once, recalling old anecdotes of their schooldays and even Ray joined in, unbending a little. Not so Trista. Dylan's good humour and amusing stories only fanned the spark of anger inside her and she would have loved to have voiced her feelings, told him just what she thought of him, but she held her tongue, not wanting to do anything to spoil Tom's and Maree's wedding. By the time everyone was called to order to begin the smörgasbörd dinner there was some degree of normality at their table.

During the eating of the delicious meal the conversation flowed freely, and if anyone noticed that Trista and to some extent Ray were a little quiet no one commented, although once or twice Gay sent a barbed look or barely veiled comment in Trista's direction.

The looks and needling Trista could cope with because as far as she was concerned if Gay Richards was interested in Dylan Ashby then she was well and truly welcome to him. But when it came to the physical closeness of him, the deepness of his voice, the way his arm or leg casually brushed hers, she found her stomach twisting in painful knots as she strove to ignore him and not flinch away as she wanted to do.

'Did you know I've got the *Blue Dancer* on the slips for repairs?' He had to ask the question twice before Trista realised he had lowered his voice to speak to her alone.

'Oh, yes, Ray ... Ray did mention that.' She set her knife and fork by her plate, knowing she couldn't face another bite.

'It wasn't as bad condition-wise as it at first appeared, so it should be ready for work again in a couple of weeks.'

'You'll be working it yourself, then?' she asked curiously.

He paused before answering. 'I'm not sure. I'll need a new crew and I was hoping Ray might be able to help me out there, suggest some reliable men.'

She looked at him in surprise, but his expression was quite serious. 'What makes you think Ray would want to help you?' She asked sharply before she could draw the words back.

Dylan's gaze flashed across to Ray, who was deep in conversation with Bill Eden, and his eyes narrowed slightly before coming back to Trista.

'The Ray Vaughan I remember would have been only to willing to help out a mate.'

A mate? Trista was so flabbergasted at his blatant effrontery she was unable to answer him. How could he expect Ray to welcome him as a friend after what he'd done? Were they all expected to simply forgive and forget? Put it down to a folly of his youth?

Fortunately, at that moment Tom's uncle called for silence and the few speeches and goodnatured teasing of the bride and groom began. After the cutting of the cake the trestle tables were cleared away and the seats arranged in a rough square so that the dancing could begin. A floor of sorts was clipped together in sections and the band struck up the strains of the bridal waltz.

As soon as the band changed tempo to a modern beat the younger members of the group flew on to the floor to begin throwing themselves around to the music. Trista sat beside Joanne and smiled with amusement at their enthusiasm.

'May I have this dance, Tris?' He was there beside her again. When she had last seen him he had been helping to stack the trestles away, and she had relaxed a little, knowing him to be otherwise occupied. Now her nerve ends were jangling again, tuned to his nearness.

'I don't think so, I'm not very good at this type of dancing.' She swallowed as her heart pounded in her throat. Her foot had been tapping to the beat and she found she really wanted to accept. If things had been different——

'Come on! Can't say I'm an expert myself, but considering my advanced age I'm regarded as passable.' He smiled that smile and Trista's resistance weakened.

'Go on, Tris, go and enjoy yourself,' put in Joanne. 'Ray will be back in a minute, so don't not dance on my account.'

Dylan took her hand and pulled her easily to her feet, keeping hold of her hand as he led her across to the makeshift dance floor.

By the time the band had finished playing the disco bracket Trista was breathless, and it wasn't totally due to the energetic dancing. The loud music and the singular style of the dance made conversation impossible, but Trista knew his dark eyes watched her. Once her eyes touched on his and the burning glow in their inky depths made her stomach turn over. After that tension-filled moment she let her gaze linger on the second top button of his cream silky shirt.

'Want to catch a brief respite?' he smiled as the band downed instruments and reached for refreshments.

Trista nodded and he led her across to their seats, sitting himself down beside her, but as she searched about for something to talk about the bride and groom appeared dressed ready to leave, for they had an hour or so's drive ahead of them to reach their honeymoon destination. Everyone gathered around, calling good wishes, teasing lightly, the bride's mother shedding a few tears as the newlyweds were given a noisy farewell. The car drove off, tin cans racketing.

'Now we can really begin the party,' remarked Tom's teenage brother, Greg, and everyone laughed, lightening the feeling of anticlimax.

'Joanne's feeling a bit tired,' Ray said to Trista as everyone moved back towards the dance floor. 'Do you mind if we go home now?'

'Of course not. I'll get my bag.' She went to move off.

'Hey, Trista, you're not leaving now, are you?' Greg rushed up to them. 'I wanted to have this dance with you.'

'Oh, I'm sorry, Greg, but Ray and Joanne are going home and I came with them.'

'No worries. We can drive you home later.' Greg was eyeing her admiringly. 'Rick and Kathy go your way. Besides, it's early yet. You can't miss the party.'

Trista opened her mouth to say she'd better go with Ray and Joanne when her brother spoke a little shortly, looking pointedly at Dylan Ashby. 'I think you should come with us, Trista.'

Ray was frowning and to Trista he sounded like a strict parent talking to a ten-year-old, and her hackles rose. Ray was getting far too domineering these days.

'I think I'll stay if you don't mind, Ray,' she said with a spark of defiance. 'I can get a lift home and I'd like to stay a little longer.'

'Trista——' Ray began, his frown deepening.

'Come on now, Ray,' Joanne broke in placatingly. 'Trista's right—it's early, and she can get someone to drop her home.'

Ray looked as though he was about to argue and then gave in, a frown still on his face as his gaze moved to Dylan, who stood silently just behind Trista. 'All right. We'll see you later, then.'

'Great! Let's go, Trista. The band's about to start up again.' Greg raced off, pulling her after him.

As he danced with the energetic abandonment of his sixteen years Trista wondered if she should be amused or irritated by his obvious admiration, for she had known Greg since he was a toddler. He was a tall good-looking boy, the youngest of the large Owen family, and as such he was a little spoilt. When the music stopped she thankfully walked to a nearby seat, deciding that young Greg was going to be in great demand with the girls when he grew up.

'Let's do the next bracket, too,' he suggested enthusiastically. 'You're a really great mover, Tris.'

'Thank you,' she replied drily, 'but I think I need to sit this one out to catch my breath. I'm an old person, you know.'

'No, you're not. You're hardly old at all,' Greg hastily reassured her. 'Shall I get you a drink?'

'I'd love one. Just Coke would be fine.' Trista sat back and looked about her as she waited for Greg to return.

'He's right, you are a great mover. For an old person, that is.' The deep amusement-tinged voice had her mind and body on full alert again as he sat down beside her, leaning back with his arms folded, his long legs stretched out in front of him. 'I thought you said you weren't very good at that type of dancing.'

'I meant I hadn't done much of it, that's all,' she said quickly, unable to stop herself slanting a look at him.

And that was a mistake, for he was watching her, the corners of his eyes crinkling up with amusement, the curve of his lips playing havoc with her heartbeats. The awareness she felt surging through her was reflected in his dark eyes.

'The next dance is mine,' he said quietly, his lowered tone vibrating through her.

'I was going to sit the next one out.' Her voice sounded strangely husky and constricted as his eyes set her aflame. Everything and everyone had begun to fade into a hazy background.

Desperately she forced herself to look away from him, and with a conflicting mixture of relief and regret she saw Greg approaching.

'I have it on good authority that the next dance will be a slow one.' Dylan had moved closer, one arm now resting along the back of her chair, and his breath stirred her hair.

'Here's your drink, Trista,' Greg's voice broke into the field of burning enticement Dylan was weaving about her.

'Thanks, Greg.' She took the glass of Coke he held out to her.

Greg eyed Dylan a trifle warily. 'Mum says the next dance will be for the oldies.' He pulled a face. 'So we can sit and talk if you like.' He sat down in the chair on the other side of Trista as the band struck up the next bracket.

'Our dance, I think,' Dylan stood up and took the glass from Trista's fingers, setting it on his chair as he pulled her to her feet. 'Excuse us.' With barely a glance at Greg he led her on to the dance floor.

'Do I detect a case of puppy love?' he asked, drawing her into his arms. 'I appear to be on the receiving end of a very black look from that cheeky young devil.'

'Greg's a nice boy,' Trista said, her concentration fixed on keeping some space between her body and Dylan's.

'Mmm, I'm sure he is.'

'You were a little rude to him.'

'Was I?' His hand slid around her, his fingers spread over the small of her back as he drew her closer. 'Then it will teach him a lesson. All's fair, and a man can't afford to let some things slip through his fingers.'

Trista flushed at his words. All's fair in love. She tilted a look up at his firm jaw. In love and war. Love she wouldn't allow herself to think about, and somehow she wouldn't like to cross Dylan in any conflict. Either way, he would make a formidable adversary.

Unconsciously her body was defying her, she realised, as she allowed herself to melt against him, and she was incapable of putting up a token resistance. And that was what she should be doing—resisting him at all costs.

But this closeness felt so good—and so right, somehow. Her body moulded itself to his as though it had been made simply for that purpose and her fingers slid across his shoulder to rest on the collar of his shirt, mere millimetres from the darkness of his hair. She wanted to slide her fingers into its thickness, but she held back, afraid of a rebuff.

Dylan put her other hand against his shirt front and now both his arms were around her as they swayed together, barely moving their feet. To Trista they were the only two people on the dance floor, and she was aflame. The clean tangy maleness of him filled her nostrils and his hard body against hers fired her already blazing senses.

'Now this is what I call dancing.' Dylan's murmured words stirred the hair at her temple and she shivered faintly, her awareness of him spiralling upwards until her heartbeats were pounding in her throat. 'Even if it does brand me as an oldie.' His voice smiled and Trista glanced up at him, her eyes bright as they met his.

He caught his breath and she felt his arms tighten almost painfully, drawing her even closer to his body so that his hard thighs, his flat stomach were pressed against hers, her breasts crushed to his silk covered chest.

'Trista.' He said her name so softly she only just caught it, and she felt the tension in him as it transmitted itself to her. And when she thought she would be unable to bear it a moment longer he relaxed a little, moving slightly away from her to swing her conventionally to the final bars of the music.

Quite a few couples were laughingly leaving the floor, but Dylan made no move to follow them, standing holding her hand waiting for the music to recommence.

'Dylan! Hi again!' Gay walked up to them, a fair-haired man in tow. Her smile was for Dylan and she totally ignored Trista. 'You haven't met Troy Aimes, have you?' She directed at Dylan.

'No, I haven't.' Dylan shook the younger man's hand.

'This is Dylan Ashby, Troy,' Gay bubbled. 'You've probably heard of him.'

'Who hasn't?' remarked Troy, looking pointedly at Trista and then to her hand where Dylan still held it. She felt the rush of scarlet wash her face.

Dylan's sharp eyes didn't miss Troy's barely disguised look of mockery and he raised an enquiring eyebrow.

'Yes, well, you haven't danced with me yet, Dylan,' Gay put in hurriedly, taking his arm possessively. 'And this is as good a time as any to remedy that. Besides,' her eyelashes fluttered, 'I've only waited twenty years to dance with the handsomest guy in school.' She turned to the young man beside her. 'You don't mind, do you, Troy? You and Trista can renew your old acquaintance.'

Dylan's gaze flashed from Troy to Trista's flushed face before he smiled at Gay. 'After such flattery how could I refuse?' he said easily as he waltzed Gay off without a backward glance.

Troy stepped forward and pulled Trista into his arms, his steps awkward as he began the dance. Trista remembered he hated old-time, once saying there was only one kind of dancing and that was disco. She looked up at him tentatively.

'We can sit down if you like,' she suggested stiltedly, recalling the disaster of their last date, the way he'd sulked, cajoled and then become downright nasty when she wouldn't agree to sleep with him. 'We don't have to dance.'

He ignored what she'd said and looked unsmilingly down at her. 'I have a feeling you played me for a fool, Trista,' he said quietly.

'What . . .? I don't know what you mean,' she stammered.

'I mean that shy little girl image you project, as though you're all innocence itself, untouched by human hands.' His lips twisted mockingly. 'You sure had me taken in!'

'Troy, please—I'd like to sit down.' Trista pushed away from him, but he held her fast and she didn't want to cause a scene.

'As I said, you sure made a fool out of me,

holding me at arm's length, leading me on and then going all prim and horrified when I tried to take what you were offering.'

'I didn't lead you on, Troy, you know I didn't,' she said firmly, her face flaming again at his implication.

'Of course you did.' He gave a soft derisive laugh. 'You only have to walk across a room and you send a guy's blood pressure up, and from where I stood Dylan Ashby was no exception. He seemed very taken with you. I wonder how you feel about him? Well, Trista, have you got the hots for him, too? It would seem so, the way you two were making love on public view.'

'You're being crude, Troy.' Trista swallowed, cringing with shame. Even knowing Troy's words were coarse couldn't make her feel any worse, for wasn't there some small shred of truth in what he said? 'We were just dancing,' she added feebly.

'Dancing? Darling, I wish you'd dance with me like that!' He swung her around and stood apart from her, but only long enough to take hold of her arm, keeping her with him as he stepped off the dance floor and strolled with seeming casualness to the outskirts of the floodlit area.

'Troy, please let me go.' She tried to pull away from him.

'Not until we talk, Trista.' He swung her into the shadows of a bushy shrub and taking her unawares, pulled her roughly into his arms, his lips finding hers as he crushed her to him.

Trista struggled against his hold, but to no avail, for he held her firmly and he was far stronger than she was. She twisted her head to the side in an effort to escape the bruising pressure of his lips.

'Troy, stop it!'

'You don't mean that so why put on such a touch-me-not little act. I only fall for that sort of thing once and I'm as good as Dylan Ashby, better probably. He is a bit long in the tooth,' he said harshly, his lips sliding wetly over her jaw. 'God, I should have done this before. I've wanted to every time I saw you,' he murmured thickly, and she caught the odour of alcohol on his breath.

'Admit it, Trista! You enjoy leading us on.' His hands fumbled for the zip at the back of her dress. 'This time you're not getting away with it. You'll see it through.'

'Troy, you're drunk——'

'Maybe,' he laughed. 'But I'm not drunk enough to let some big reputation playboy come back and take what should have been mine.'

Panic began to rise inside Trista and she forced herself to be calm. Pretending to relax against him, she slid her hands around his neck and moved her fingers in his hair. Then, taking hold of a handful, she pulled it hard.

'Ouch! You little bitch!' he snarled through clenched teeth, his arms falling from around her to rub his tender scalp.

'If you touch me again, Troy, I'll ... I'll scream!' Trista got out as she took a couple of steps away from him.

Troy regarded her angrily, his eyes appearing to glitter in the semi-darkness as he smoothed his hair.

'I was right, wasn't I, Trista,' he sneered,

'when I said you were your mother's daughter?
I've heard she was the biggest tease around. Is
this how she worked, too? Lead them on and
drop them cold?'

Trista gasped, the familiar pain clutching at her,
and she drew a steadying breath. 'I think you've
said enough, Troy. Now, please, leave me alone.'

'Oh, I'll do that all right. I wouldn't touch you
with a ten-foot pole. I should have had more
sense!' He straightened his tie. 'What kind of
woman are you, Trista, making it with a guy
who's laid your mother?' He gave a harsh laugh.
'Although it should be quite interesting for him,
comparing.'

Trista's hand shot up to connect with his face.
'How dare you say that? You're sick, Troy
Aimes! Now get out of my sight! I never want to
see you again!' She pressed her hand to her
stomach, feeling nauseated to her very soul.

'The same goes for me, Trista. I hope the three
of you will be very happy,' he threw over his
shoulder as he strode away, leaving her standing
in the shadows.

Two large tears trickled down Trista's cheeks
and her legs felt like jelly. How could Troy even
think that, let alone say it? That she could——
Was that what everyone was thinking? Was it in
their minds as they watched her talking to Dylan
Ashby, dancing with him? Were they all
remembering his liaison with her mother?

Oh, God! She had to get out of here before she
completely broke down. Ray was right—she
should have gone home with them instead of
trying to pretend she belonged, that she could
take a party, any party, in her stride. Sooner or

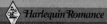

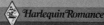

LOVE BEYOND REASON
There was a surprise in store for Amy!

Amy had thought nothing could be as perfect as the days she had shared with Vic Hoyt in New York City—before he took off for his Peace Corps assignment in Kenya.

Impulsively, Amy decided to follow. She was shocked to find Vic established in his new life... and interested in a new girl friend.

Amy faced a choice: be smart and go home... or stay and fight for the only man she would ever love.

MAN OF POWER
Sara took her role seriously

Although Sara had already planned her escape from the subservient position in which her father's death had placed her, Morgan Haldane's timely appearance had definitely made it easier.

All Morgan had asked in return was that she pose as his fiancée. He'd confessed to needing protection from his partner's wife, Louise, and that part of Sara's job proved easy.

But unfortunately for Sara's heart, Morgan hadn't told her about Monique...

THE LEO MAN
"He's every bit as sexy as his father!"

Her grandmother thought that description would appeal to Rowan, but Rowan was determined to avoid any friendship with the arrogant James Fraser.

Aboard his luxury yacht, that wasn't easy. When they were all shipwrecked on a tropical island, it proved impossible.

And besides, if it weren't for James, none of them would be alive. Rowan was confused. Was it merely gratitude that she now felt for this strong and rugged man?

THE WINDS OF WINTER
She'd had so much— now she had nothing

Anne didn't dwell on it, but the pain was still with her—the double-edged pain of grief and rejection.

It had greatly altered her; Anne barely resembled the girl who four years earlier had left her husband, David. He probably wouldn't even recognize her—especially with another name.

Anne made up her mind. She just had to go to his house to discover if what she suspected was true...

Your Romantic Adventure Starts Here.

These FOUR free Harlequin Romance novels allow you to enter the world of romance, love and desire. As a member of the Harlequin Home Subscription Plan, you can continue to experience all the moods of love. You'll be inspired by moments so real...so moving...you won't want them to end. So start your own Harlequin Romance adventure by returning the reply card below. <u>DO IT TODAY!</u>

EXTRA BONUS
MAIL YOUR ORDER
TODAY AND GET A
FREE COSMETIC BAG
FROM HARLEQUIN.

later it always happened. There would be the inevitable mention of her mother, if only inadvertently. She realised she was super-sensitive about it and she'd tried so hard to reason with herself, to get it into perspective. But it was always there. Once Ray had tried to assure her that people forget but then someone like Troy Aimes brought it all back.

Taking a deep breath, she wiped the telltale dampness from her eyes and began to compose herself. She'd find Tom's mother, say her goodbyes and take a taxi home.

'Trista!'

She jumped as a figure materialized beside her.

'Oh, Greg! You . . . you startled me!'

'Sorry. What are you doing in the dark? Come and dance again?'

'No, thanks, Greg. I'm a little tired, so I think I'll call it a night.'

'Hey, it's too early for that.' He walked with her as she headed over to collect her handbag. 'Besides, Rick and Kathy aren't ready to go yet. Rick's gone to pick up another keg.'

'That doesn't matter. I can call a taxi.'

'Aw, Trista!' he moaned exaggeratedly, 'I was looking forward to having another dance with you. Won't you stay?'

'What are you pressuring Trista about, Greg?' His mother joined them.

'Trista was going to go home, but I want her to stay and dance,' he frowned, not used to not getting his own way.

'If Trista wants to go she's entitled to go,' smiled his mother. 'Anyway, your father needs a hand over there with some chairs.'

'Oh, Mum!'

'Go on now, there's a good boy.'

'I'm not a boy,' he went off muttering to himself.

The older woman turned back to Trista. 'Do you really want to go home now, love, or was Greg making a nuisance of himself? You seemed to be having such a good time and I was pleased to see you enjoying yourself so much.'

'Oh, I was, and Greg wasn't any trouble, really. It was a lovely wedding, but I'm just a little tired. May I use your telephone to call a taxi?'

'Well, of course, if you're sure you want to go home. Come on inside.' Greg's mother turned to lead her into the house.

'No need for the taxi, Mrs Owen. I was about to leave myself, so I'll drop Trista home. After all, we are neighbours.'

CHAPTER SIX

Tom's mother looked a little taken aback, her glance going to Trista before she commented.

'If I may?' Dylan added with that same magnetising smile, and the older woman had no defence against his charm.

'There, that solves the taxi problem, Trista.'

'Yes,' Trista agreed reluctantly. How she wished she could firmly decline his offer! But of course she didn't, because part of her really wanted to accept anyway so she was fighting herself again where Dylan Ashby was concerned. Besides, what harm could it do? It was only a five or six-minute journey. She quickly pushed thoughts of Ray's displeasure to the back of her mind. 'Thank you for the lovely evening. I've enjoyed it.' She managed to keep her voice steady as she spoke to Mrs Owen.

'And I second that,' added Dylan. 'Thanks for the invitation. I wouldn't have missed being part of Tom's big day.'

'And Tom was so pleased you could come,' beamed Mrs Owen. 'You were such good friends, the three of you. Tom and Ray missed you when you——' Her eyes dropped in embarrassment as she realised she had almost mentioned a subject which Trista would find painful. 'When you left,' she finished quickly.

'The Three Mischiefers, Tom's father called us, and looking back it was an apt title,' Dylan laughed easily. 'We certainly got up to some pranks in our time!'

'That you did!' Mrs Owen laughed with him, obviously glad to be over an uncomfortable moment.

'Well, we'll say goodnight.' He put his arm casually around Trista's waist. 'Ready to go?' he asked her solicitously.

She nodded, added her goodbyes to his, and once again she found herself sitting back in the luxurious comfort of the silver-grey Mazda with Dylan Ashby beside her.

He had shed his jacket and tie and folded back the cuffs of his shirt, and his tanned wrists and forearms held her almost mesmerised as he settled in the car beside her.

'What upset you, Trista?' he asked out of the blue.

She had made no attempt at conversation as he drove homewards and she had been thinking that Dylan must also be feeling disinclined to talk, so she was somewhat taken aback, as much by the sudden sound of his voice as his question.

'Upset? What ... what makes you think I'm upset?' she stammered, her hand going nervously to her throat in an unconscious effort to ease her constricted breathing.

'One minute you were happily dancing and the next you want to rush off home.'

'I was a little tired, that's all. I was ready to call it a night,' Her excuses sounded feeble and unconvincing.

'Was I stepping on Aimes' toes as well as young Greg's?' he asked quietly, and Trista gasped a breath.

'No, of course not! There's nothing between Troy and me.'

'He appeared to be just a little put out about something, especially after your little stroll in the moonlight.'

'Stroll in the—— We did not go strolling in the moonlight! And it's hardly your business if we did,' she finished, glad of the dimness of the car's interior as she felt her face flush red. 'We ... we were just talking,' she finished lamely, knowing as she said it it only made it sound worse.

'What did you argue about?'

'Argue? We ... we simply ... talked. Troy doesn't care for old-time dancing.'

'I see.' His tone said he saw far more than she was admitting to, and Trista felt a spurt of guilt-based anger. He had no right to cross examine her about Troy.

'There's no need to drive right down to my house,' she said evenly as they turned into the top end of their street. 'I can walk across the road from your place.'

Surprisingly, for she expected an argument, he took her at her word and stopped the car in the driveway of the Ashby house, which was roughly similar to the Vaughans' and of the same vintage. Switching off the ignition, he walked around the car to open her door for her and she stepped out on to the concrete pathway. At least Ray wouldn't see his car and know who had driven her home.

'Thank you for the lift.' Her words sounded strangely stilted and her heart was hammering as she turned to walk away. 'Goodnight.'

Strong fingers circled her arm as Dylan fell into step beside her, and she stopped.

'There's no need for you to come across the road with me. It's quite moonlight.'

'I offered to see you home, Trista, and I will,' he said firmly, and when she still hesitated he gave an amusedly exasperated laugh. 'Come on, don't deny me my moment of gallantry!'

The moonlight was almost bright enough to discern colours, the metal of the road surface, the greens of the trees, so they had no difficulty seeing their way diagonally across the street. A large flowering gum shielded part of the house from the road on the top side and as they neared the open double gates Trista found herself walking on tiptoe. If Ray should see Dylan escorting her home he would be far from pleased.

'Which entrance do you use, front or back?' Dylan's voice seemed to explode in the semi-darkness and she jumped.

'The . . . the back,' she whispered, and led the way along the path to her door. There was an entrance to her flat through the garage at the front, but she usually used the door into the kitchen.

'This is it.' She stopped at the corner and Dylan stepped past her to look up towards the back stairs.

'Where's your key? I'll go first.'

'I don't mean upstairs, I go in here.' She indicated the yellow door and began fumbling in her bag for her key. 'I have the flat downstairs and Ray and Joanne live in the house.'

Her fingers found the bunch of keys and she turned towards the full moon's light to pick out the door key. Her hand was shaking as she tried to insert the key in the lock and Dylan's fingers closed over hers, moving the key into the slot in one precise movement. He swung the door open and his hand felt for the light switch. The brightness cascaded out on to the path, throwing the moonlit garden into a sudden blackness, and Trista stepped inside, turning back to bid him goodnight.

'Thank you for seeing me home,' she said formally, and one corner of his mouth lifted in a crooked smile.

'My pleasure,' he replied, his eyes going past her into the kitchen. 'I see you've done the old flat up. Your father used to use it as a work area and storeroom, didn't he?'

'Yes.' Trista moved a little to the side so that he could see more of the room. 'It's fairly small, but it suits me very well.' Her eyes met his and the air about her seemed to grow heavier, hotter. Why didn't he leave? He'd done his chivalrous duty. But she wanted him to stay.

'Would you . . . would you like a cup of coffee?' The words were out before she consciously thought them, and then it was too late to draw them back. She could have bitten off her tongue at her foolishness. Every moment she spent with him was simply playing with fire, a fire that was always on the very verge of fulminating. Of course, he would refuse.

'I'd love one,' he smiled, and all her self-admonishment for making that offer died a very quick death. That moment of anger as they drove home was forgotten as a fountain of inner pleasure rose and blossomed into a smile that lit her face. 'Black without sugar,' he added softly after a moment.

Slightly flushed, Trista stood back for him to enter and he stepped inside closing the door behind him. She set her bag on the table and crossed to the sink to fill the electric kettle. His tallness dwarfed what had been a reasonably fair-sized kitchen and he walked across to the small divider that separated the kitchen from the living-room.

Trista tried to see it through his eyes, the pale walls and thick carpet, the dark brown cushions on the light pine chairs, the seascapes on the wall, scenes from along Whaler's Way painted in oils by a local artist. As she set out two coffee mugs he walked into the other half of the room to stand examining the paintings.

'Cape Carnot, Topgallant Cliffs, Theakstone's Crevasse and Cape Wiles,' he said reflectively. 'There's something dangerously exciting about that section of the coast.' He turned back to her. 'At least, I've always thought so.'

Trista poured boiling water on to the coffee granules and carried the two mugs into the living-room on a small tray. Setting the tray on the low occasional table she sat down on the two seater lounge chair.

'I know what you mean. It's beautiful but treacherous.' She handed him his coffee and he took it almost absently. 'The sea's so beautifully blue you don't at first realise that the white foam swirling about the reefs is so dangerous to ships.'

Dylan was still looking at the paintings and Trista could study his profile, allowing herself the luxury of taking in each strong feature . . . All the while knowing she was launching herself into seas just as dangerous as the waters around Liguanea Island and Cape Carnot.

'When I was a boy I used to try to imagine how Matthew Flinders and all those other unnamed sailors felt sailing in unknown waters, not knowing what to expect, when a hidden reef might rip open the bottom of the boat, and I remember it gave me goosebumps just thinking about it.'

Trista smiled involuntarily and he raised an eyebrow.

'It's true.'

'Oh, I didn't mean to imply I didn't believe you. It's just hard to imagine you——' she stopped speaking as he sat down beside her on the lounge chair, so close, far too close.

'As a child or as a child with goosebumps?' He laughed softly.

'A little of both, I guess.'

'Well, I was and I did.' He sipped his coffee. 'Of course, it was some time before you arrived on the scene.'

His eyes crinkled at the corners as he smiled, and Trista set her coffee mug virtually untouched on the tray, and clasped her hands together in her lap. His nearness was having the now familiar effect on her and she wished she could move to another chair, put some space between them.

'I must get out to Whaler's Way again to renew my acquaintance with it.'

She could feel his eyes on her and her body began to tingle with awareness.

'Want to come with me on my pilgrimage, Tris?' he asked quietly, his tone a sensual assault on her.

'Oh, I don't think I . . . well, I work, so I don't get a lot of free time,' she stammered feebly.

'Surely even you have a day of rest, or does Trent keep you shackled to your desk?' Dylan laughed softly, teasing Trista's senses even more.

'Of course not. But ...' She couldn't look at him now, afraid of what he might see in her eyes, and she felt naïve and foolish.

His fingers took hold of her chin and he gently turned her face towards him. 'But?' he questioned softly, his eyes now capturing hers, holding her enmeshed in their dark depths.

'Well, I'm ... I'm sure you don't want me tagging along.' She tried for lightness, but her mouth had gone suddenly dry. 'Ray said you and he used to give me short shrift when I was a little girl and you went anywhere.' Her soft laugh sounded forced and she nervously moistened her dry lips with the tip of her tongue.

A nerve at the corner of his mouth began to beat and she couldn't tear her eyes away from its steady pulsation, for it seemed her heart was thudding loudly in unison. The light hold of his fingers on her chin changed, seemed to tighten, although she felt no added physical pressure and all at once the tense awareness appeared to fill the room, headily combustible. The silence screamed between them and her eyes went back to his, her own arousal reflected in the inky depths of his.

'But you're not a little girl any longer,' he said at last, so softly that she barely caught it. 'It might be better if you were,' he added brokenly as his lips descended to claim hers.

If he had forced a passion-filled assault upon her she would have instinctively fought him all the way, but he didn't. His lips gently caressed, coaxed, and aroused, stirring her senses until her need of him escaped from the tight hold she had had on it and began to rise in tiny waves from the pit of her stomach, rushing upwards to engulf her. Her body was in control now, her conscious thought so easily consumed to nothingness.

His teeth nibbled her bottom lip, sending erotic shivers of desire coursing through her, and she moaned softly, moving involuntarily closer to him. His fingertips teased her jawline, gliding into the softness of her hair, the pad of his thumb tantalising the sensitive area around her earlobe.

Her own fingers found the buttons of his shirt, slid inside over the hardness of his midriff. How she loved the feel of him, exalted in the heavy beats of his heart beneath her hand.

'God, Trista! What you do to me!' he groaned as he sought the savour of her lips again, covering her mouth with his, enmeshing her, evoking a response that matched the passion that so obviously had hold of him.

Their bodies strained together, her breasts crushed against the hardness of his chest as he rained kisses on her face, her forehead, her eyes, her nose, to claim her lips again, tasting the sweetness within as she opened her mouth beneath the pressure of his.

Never had Trista known such ignitable passion. No one had ever kissed her like this, casting her inhibitions to the four winds, demanding and receiving a response she gave spontaneously without a shred of restraint. No one had ever made her feel the way Dylan did, lifting her upwards, setting her body aflame, driving any thought of repulsion from her like leaves before a sea breeze.

Her body was simply tuned to his melody, and his alone. His hands played the only notes she had ever heard, and their mutual arousal rose about them like some glorious symphony.

Now his fingers teased the length of her backbone through the soft green crêpe of her dress, a barrier, returned to tempt the bare skin of her shoulders. She was scarcely aware of his fingers finding the zip at the back of her dress, sliding it easily downwards and then his cool fingers touched her heated skin moving along the shallow valley of her spine, releasing an even greater cascade of wanting to wash over her.

His lips nuzzled the softness of her throat, her shoulder, exciting shivers of delight, and she let her hands encircle the hardness of his body beneath his shirt, luxuriating in the feel of his firm muscles moving as he moved.

His hand followed the curve of her ribcage, pushing aside her dress so that he could cup one full naked breast, his fingers finding and caressing an erect nipple. Trista moaned his name as the sensations he was creating carried her higher, had her straining closer to him, lost now as he showed her a self-awareness she had never dreamed existed within her.

Her fingers twined in his dark hair, bound him to her, as his lips found the valley between her breasts, scaled one taut pinacle to close on a rosy peak. She softly sighed his name and his mouth left her breast to find her lips again.

He gently pushed her back on to the couch, his hard body following hers, capturing her beneath him, their legs entwined. He was as aroused as she was, their closeness making that so overtly obvious, and she exalted in the fact that he was wanting her as much as she wanted him, loved him, wanted him to love her, to make love to her. And she knew it was all there in her eyes. At that precise moment she couldn't even begin to hide it from him if he chose to look.

Caressing the hard smoothness of his shoulder, she ran her tonguetip to his earlobe, her eyelashes falling to shield that so betraying expression in her eyes. 'Dylan?' she murmured softly.

'Mmm?'

'Make love to me.'

His lips continued to blaze a trail of fire over first one breast and then the other.

'No one ever made me feel like this before. Make love to me,' she whispered, not recognising the seductive quality in her voice and his lips stilled.

Pushing himself up on his arms, Dylan gazed down into her eyes, catching his breath at the message he read there—her arousal, her inexperience.

'Oh, Trista!' he groaned softly, and sat up, running a hand over the hardness of his jaw. 'Trista!'

'Dylan, what . . . what's the matter? Don't you want to make love to me?'

He turned back to her then, the fire blazing in his own eyes. 'Want to? I want to make love to you like crazy, but you look——' He stood up and began to tuck his shirt back into his pants, not trying to disguise the fact that he was as aroused as she was. 'You look just like——' He shook his head and picked up their now cold coffee mugs and strode with them into the kitchen.

As he moved away Trista turned icy cold. Hastily she sat up, blushing shamefully at her nakedness and quickly adjusted her dress, sliding the zip upwards as she struggled to her feet. How could she have lost control so easily?

Looking up, she saw he had returned to the room, had rebuttoned his shirt and was standing running a hand over his tossled hair. She cringed with self-disgust.

'Dylan, I'm sorry, I——' She hung her head and with a muffled curse he strode across to wrap her in his arms.

'I'm the one who should be sorry. I had no right to start that.' His arms tightened about her. 'When I came across to see you home I thought I could handle the situation, keep my hands off you, but now we know I failed miserably at that.' His hands moved to cup her face. 'God knows, I've wanted to make love to you again ever since that day on Winters Hill.' His lips brushed her cheek and, unable to deny herself, Trista turned her head, her mouth seeking his.

For a few seconds his lips were cool, but just as suddenly he crushed her tightly against him, kissing her almost desperately. And then she was standing apart from him and he was striding towards the door, pausing on the threshold to turn back to face her. His eyes were dark pools as he went to say more, then stopped, and with a quick goodnight the door was closed and he had gone.

For immeasurable moments Trista stood where he had left her, her body as still as a statue, transfixed, glued to the spot. And she felt somehow bereft, as though part of her had been torn away.

Wrapping her arms about her body, she tried to calm her still clamouring senses, and then the full import of what she had almost done hit her like a hammer blow. For the first time in her life she had almost allowed a man to make love to her. Her lips twisted self-derisively. Allowed? More like begged, didn't she mean? She had all but begged Dylan Ashby to make love to her. Dylan Ashby!

Trista sank down on to the couch and covered her face with her hands. Dylan Ashby. She'd allowed Dylan Ashby to kiss her, to caress her, to touch her body far more intimately than any other man had done, than she'd ever wanted any other man to touch her.

God! Troy had been right. Like mother, like daughter. What kind of woman was she to want that particular man to make love to her, a man who had also made love to her own mother? And what was it Dylan had said? 'You look just like——!' Just like who? Who else but her mother?

She stood up and crossed to the divider, pulling open the bottom drawer with fumbling fingers. The framed photograph was there beneath a pile of table linen, and she drew it out. Her mother's likeness smiled innocently up at her. It was the only photograph of her mother she had ever seen, and she had only found it by chance tucked away in the back of a drawer when she was clearing through her father's things after his death. Even Ray didn't know she'd kept it.

Was she like this woman who had caused them all such pain? Trista couldn't see any resemblance. Perhaps there was a little similarity about the eyes. Angela Vaughan was much fairer, her lips turned up in a soft smile.

The face in the photograph was no less beautiful than the rather ethereal picture Trista had carried in her childhood memories. No! She thrust the photograph back into the drawer. No, she wasn't like her mother, not in any way. No matter what Troy Aimes or Dylan Ashby or the whole world said, she could never believe she was at all like the beautiful but shallow Angela Vaughan who had sacrificed her husband and children for what had obviously been a brief physical fling.

'Trista!' Joanne's call from the kitchen doorway brought Trista out of her hunched-over misery.

She had tossed restlessly when she had finally crawled into bed the night before, her emotions soaring from depression to agonised guilt to a wondrous knowledge of the discovery of her own sexuality. And it was Dylan Ashby who had shown her just how responsive she could be. Until last night she hadn't suspected she could respond to a man so wholly, so irrevocably.

Remembering the shyness of her first kisses, the tenative pressure of adolescent lips, she could scarcely believe that she had actually experienced such rapture when Dylan had kissed and caressed her. And since those first naïve kisses, stolen at a school dance, she had not exactly added much to her experience, not pleasantly anyway. On both occasions her dealings with the opposite sex had ended disastrously, leaving her emotionally raw and hurt.

Her first date when she returned to Port Lincoln from boarding school had been with Chris Jones. She met him at a party and she had been so pleased and excited when he had singled her out. Chris was quite nice-looking and at twenty-two had seemed so grown-up to her seventeen years. They had gone to barbecues with other young people and to the movies and dances.

At first Trista had enjoyed his light goodnight kisses, but as they became more urgent with each date she had begun to move away from him. On their last evening together he had been even more persistent, and then he had grown angry, demanding what was wrong with her, telling her everyone did it. Weren't these liberated times and not the Dark Ages?

Still Trista had held back, knowing that making love completely should be far more special than the way Chris meant it to be. And she'd tried to explain this to him, but he'd only grown more belligerent. Who was she to be so choosy anyway? With a mother like hers he thought she'd have been only too willing, especially as he'd done the right thing by her, taken her out to places and kept his hands off her until after they'd got to know each other. Didn't she know that a guy expected more than a little-girl peck on the cheek?

Trista had shrunk back in the seat, shaking her head emphatically. She didn't believe in sex simply for the sake of it. She wasn't that type of girl. Chris had laughed cruelly at that. What other type was there? he sneered, then slid closer again. She was old-fashioned. He could teach her all about life, how to treat a man. Trista pushed at him again, a sob catching in her throat, and Chris had thrust her away from him. She should take a leaf out of her mother's book, he snarled as he started the car. By all accounts she really knew what a man liked and wanted, and he'd no time to waste on shrinking little virgins. What a let-down she was, what with her mother and all!

'Not still dozing, were you?' Joanne asked as she came inside and lowered herself on to the lounge chair opposite Trista.

'No, not really. I just couldn't seem to sleep last night.' Trista rubbed her gritty eyes.

'You do look a bit seedy,' smiled Joanne, and Trista grimaced.

'Thanks. How are you feeling today?' she changed the subject.

'I'm fine. Why couldn't you sleep?' pursued Joanne, not to be sidetracked.

'Just a little keyed up, I guess. I'll have an early night tonight to catch up. What did you think of the wedding?' Trista attempted to steer the conversation into safer channels.

'Lovely, wasn't it? Maree's a nice girl, just right for Tom, and both families seem happy about it all. Did we miss anything leaving early?'

'No. No, I don't think so.' Trista made an effort to change the position of her cushion so that she wouldn't have to meet her sister-in-law's candid gaze. 'I didn't stay long after you left.'

'Did you have a dance?' Joanne asked.

'Yes, a very energetic one with young Greg.' Trista tried to laugh easily, but it sounded forced even to her ears.

'Trista, I'm sorry Ray came the heavy big brother last night,' Joanne frowned. 'I took him to task over it when we came home. I guess he finds it hard to realise you're grown-up and don't need him guarding you like an over-protective father.'

'That's all right, I understand.' Trista shrugged. 'I admit Ray ordering me home partly made me decide to stay. It was childish of me too, but at the time he rubbed me the wrong way.'

Joanne patted her hand. 'At least you had a nice night out. You know, you should get out more.'

'Oh, I'm okay, Joanne—really.' Trista began.

'Now I'm doing it, aren't I?' Joanne laughed. 'I hope when the baby arrives it might put an end to our frustrated parents complex where you're concerned, love.'

Trista laughed with Joanne. 'I appreciate the fact that you care. It's nice to be part of a family that does.' She sobered. 'If it hadn't been for Ray I guess I would have had a very lonely childhood.'

'Tris, if I'm stepping on sacred ground just tell me to button my lip, but do you remember your mother? I was absolutely flabbergasted to find out she was alive. Ray never mentioned her before, and neither have you.'

'I don't remember her very well, only brief incidents here and there. I suppose I have kind of fairytale memories, not quite real. It was a long time ago.' Trista stood up and paced restlessly across the floor.

'Dylan Ashby was something of a shock,' Joanne remarked softly. 'Not at all what I imagined.'

'Oh! In . . . In what way? Was he not what you imagined, I mean?' Trista's breathing had shallowed and she was glad she had her back to the other girl, for she felt the colour flood her face.

'Well, he's younger, for a start. I'd not thought of him being Ray's age.' Joanne paused and Trista could feel her eyes on her back. 'He's very attractive, don't you think?'

'I suppose so.' Trista drew a swift steadying breath to regain her composure before turning around to face Joanne again. 'Very typically tall, dark and handsome,' she quipped with a shrug.

'Very! I noticed he was on the receiving end of quite a few admiring looks yesterday afternoon, especially from Gay Richards. She was all but drooling over him!' Joanne grinned. 'However, he seemed to handle it all pretty well.'

'He's probably had lots of practice,' Trista retorted a trifle bitterly, and Joanne sighed.

'It's such a pity about it all, though. He was so absolutely charming at dinner. I mean, he couldn't have been nicer to talk to, even if Ray was all stiff and frosty.' Joanne glanced at the set expression on Trista's face. 'Look, I'm sorry, Tris, I'm upsetting you, and I have to admit that after what happened I can't say I blame Ray being antagonistic towards him, but,' she raised her hands and let them fall, 'he just doesn't fit the type of person who'd—well, run off with someone else's wife. I mean, I just can't see it.'

'I think he's very plausible. He'd have to be, to talk someone into leaving everything to run off with him, wouldn't he?' Trista doused a persistent spurt of emotions that rose to remind her just how deceptive Dylan had been. Hadn't she experienced the ease with which he could manoeuvre a woman into his arms?

'He was only young—what, about eighteen? That's such an intense age. Maybe he—' Joanne stopped and shook her head. 'What the heck, it's all in the past, and no amount of psychoanalysis will change it or help any.' She sighed loudly. 'What I'm really trying to get around to saying is that I rather think Dylan Ashby has an eye for you, Tris, and your overbearing brother thinks so too. Hence this supposedly girl-to-girl chat Ray's made me promise to have with you, to warn you off Dylan,' Joanne finished in a rush.

Trista's face flushed a dull red.

'But of course I'm not going to warn you off him,' continued Joanne, 'because I think you're old enough to know what you're doing.'

Trista swallowed guiltily.

'Anyway, let's change the subject. How about a cup of tea?' Joanne smiled, and Trista stood up thankfully. A moment longer over that particular conversation and she had a feeling she would have broken down and made a huge fool of herself in front of her sister-in-law. And if Ray found out—well, it would hardly make the situation any better.

They were in the kitchen and Trista was washing their cups and saucers when firm footsteps sounded along the concrete pathway beside the house. Trista and Joanne turned towards the door as Dylan Ashby appeared, his large frame filling the open doorway.

'Hi there!' he greeted them easily. 'I called to see if Ray was home.'

Joanne shot a swift glance at Trista before answering. 'No, he's not at the moment. He's down at the boat. I'm not sure when he'll be home.'

'Not to worry. I just wanted to discuss a few aspects of the tuna fishing industry with him, catch up on recent developments.' His dark eyes went to Trista as she dried her hands on a towel. 'Which leaves me with a free afternoon. Would you both care to come out to Whaler's Way for a drive?' he asked.

'I don't think I will, thanks,' Joanne replied quickly. 'I was planning on having a nice long rest this afternoon.'

'And I should keep Joanne company,' Trista began.

'No need for that, love, if you want to go along with Dylan. I'll be fine,' Joanne smiled cheerfully.

If you want to go with Dylan? The words raced around in Trista's head. If she wanted to. God— one part of her desperately wanted to be with him, but to give in to that wanting would be downright reckless. They'd be alone together again, and that must be avoided at all cost.

'How about it, Trista?' He was smiling at her and she felt her defences begin to weaken again. 'It's over fifteen years, I'd say, since I've been near that part of the coastline and it's ideal weather today, not too hot and not too windy.'

CHAPTER SEVEN

As it followed the coastline of Proper Bay the Sleaford Road passed the tuna processing factories that provided jobs for many of the Port Lincolnites. Heading out along the road, Dylan drove the Mazda with his usual effortless expertise, while seated beside him Trista kept her eyes glued on the passing scenery, countryside she knew almost by heart.

She wouldn't, couldn't allow herself to look at Dylan. The night before lived too vividly in her mind for her to be able to relax with him. She still didn't quite know how she had let herself be talked into coming with him, and Joanne's attitude hadn't helped. Go along if you want to, Tris, she'd said, and it had only taken one of Dylan's smiles to have her falling all over herself to agree to his plans. And now here she sat all tense and tongue-tied. She couldn't for the life of her think of a thing to say to break the silence that had fallen between them from the moment Joanne had seen them off in the car.

'Ah! I thought this sealed road was too good to be true,' Dylan remarked as the metal-surfaced road gave way to a somewhat corrugated ironstone gravel. He wound up his window to keep out the cloud of dust that was being stirred up by the car.

'What about the gate? I think you need a key to go into Whaler's Way,' Trista told him, frowning.

It was years since she'd been any further south than Sleaford Bay.

'I have that.' He tapped his pocket. 'I picked it up this morning in the hope that I could talk you into coming with me.' He turned slightly to smile at her, and she involuntarily smiled back at him.

'You could have come alone,' she said as some of his easy amiability began to calm her clamouring nerve-ends.

'I could have, but I wanted you to come with me, Tris,' he replied quietly.

The tension grew again in the cabin and Trista flushed hotly, his softly spoken words tugging at her senses. Even the sound of his voice using that particular tone could have her body crying out to be moulded close against him, his strong arms holding her safely.

And he said he'd wanted her to come with him to revisit an old haunt. Her heart began to sing and suddenly the afternoon ahead of them, just Dylan and herself, took on the rosiest of hues. The sea on their left seemed to Trista to be incredibly bluer, the dry stunted vegetation coated in fine dust was impossibly greener, and a total sense of wellbeing washed over her.

Nothing must mar this afternoon, not thoughts of Ray's displeasure—and not those brutal memories of her mother. This afternoon was going to be hers and nothing was going to spoil it.

Dylan climbed out of the car and walked back to close the gate behind them at the entrance to Whaler's Way. The dirt road was relatively smooth, and he turned the car into a layby and switched off the engine.

'Let's have a closer look,' he suggested, and opened the door.

The wind whipped Trista's hair back from her face as she walked beside Dylan towards the cliff edge. The sea was a deep unfathomable blue pounding with white anger on the rocks of the ragged reddish-brown coastline. From where they stood they could see the jagged rock-protected translucency of the Swimming Hole, constructed by nature itself and tucked in against the cliff shore.

They slipped into an easy companionship as they talked together, recalling the whaling days, now etched in the past, with the old Sleaford Bay Whaling Station at Fishery Bay a reminder of those adventure-filled times. Dylan regaled her with stories of those bygone days, stories her father had told him and Ray on their frequent fishing trips when they were boys. It was a side of her father Trista had never seen, for to her he had always seemed remote, a bitter and dissatisfied man.

Back in the car they drove southwards to Cape Wiles, named by Matthew Flinders in 1802. Trista leaned gingerly on the safety rail to gaze down into the water hundreds of feet below. Huge rocky chunks appeared to have been sliced away from the mainland to sit as island sentinels taking the brunt of the crashing ocean currents.

In the relative calm between the islands and the mainland a grey rubber dinghy bobbed on the swells while two skin-divers in dark wet-suits glided along through the clear turquoise water like a couple of sleek fish. Somehow on this ruggedly spectacular coastline it was comforting to know they weren't alone.

They turned to retrace their steps to the car, pausing to gaze at Topgallant Cliffs which climbed striatedly to four hundred feet. Trista shivered and was thankful of Dylan's strong fingers on her arm as they followed the foot-worn path.

Continuing on, they explored each little side-track, the relative calm of Groper Bay, the sharp slices of the crevasses, until Dylan stopped the car overlooking Cape Carnot. Some way offshore was Liguanea Island with the white foam of the reefs between it and the mainland.

Picking their way over the limestone-strewn ground, they walked down closer to the cape, past the lifebuoy and the warning sign that told of freak waves that could so easily sweep an unwary sightseer from the rocks into the churning ocean. From the water emerged deceptively flat shelf-like rocks that built up to higher ground. As they watched a wave smashed on the shelf behind the pile of sharp boulders, sending sea-spray high into the air to subside and surge around the point gushing into the crevasses, trying to climb ever higher, falling back in a mêlée of brownish foam.

Sitting back on the rocky seats, they watched the sea demonstrate its power and neither spoke, both content to sit and watch, caught in the majesty of the spectacular scene. The sunlight sparkled on the jets of spray rainbowing across the backdrop of the cobalt sky.

'Feel like a cup of coffee?' Dylan was the first to break the silence and Trista glanced at him in surprise. He gave her a crooked smile that started a growing glow in the pit of her stomach. 'Be back in a minute.'

He returned with a thermos of coffee and a rug which he spread out on a flat piece of ground in front of a rocky outcrop so that they could use the rocks as a backrest. When they were seated side by side he poured some steaming coffee into one of the two unbreakable mugs and passed it to her. Their fingers touched and held, joined around the coffee mug, and Dylan's eyes flared with a coal-black flame.

Simply take the offered coffee, Trista told herself, her breathing quickening. Make some innocuous remark about the scene spread out before them or about the weather. Bring the thickening atmosphere back to normal. But she couldn't somehow manage to do it. Her vocal chords had ceased to function and her breath was caught painfully somewhere in her chest.

She felt his eyes burning her where they touched on her hot skin and her own eyes slid over his firm jaw, lingered on the so sensual curve of his lips, before meeting his gaze. Her eyes were drawn compellingly to his and once her gaze had met his she was totally incapable of looking away. She was lost, drowning in water as turbulent, as volatile as Old Smoky Bombora in the sea on their right.

The tension built up about them, and just when Trista thought she would be unable to bear it a moment longer Dylan drew his hand from the mug, breaking that electrifying contact, freeing the breath that had caught in Trista's chest. She glanced surreptitiously at Dylan's averted profile, saw the rigidity in the way he held his head as he poured his own coffee.

Neither tried to break the silence. They drank

their coffee, Trista without tasting it, still very much aware of the tense ambiance of tinder-dry feelings that only awaited one tiny spark to set a raging inferno engulfing them. Her hand began to tremble and she hurriedly put her coffee mug down beside her on the rocks, holding her hands together in her lap. She had to say something—anything.

'The painting in my living-room captures this scene quite truly, doesn't it?' she remarked tentatively, finding her voice at last, for all that it was somewhat thin and wavering.

'Yes, it does,' he agreed. 'Can't say I've heard of the fellow who painted it. Is he a local?'

Trista's tightened muscles relaxed just a little. 'He lives at Coffin Bay. I think he said he came over from Adelaide ten years ago. He teaches art at the high school.'

Dylan nodded absently as he swirled what remained of his coffee in his mug. 'You used to enjoy painting, as I remember.' He laughed softly. 'Do you still do those flattering portraits?'

'No. I guess I wasn't exactly another Picasso, but I did like doing it. Ray still has the one I painted of you two when you caught that big snapper the day you played hookey from school.'

'So you do remember.' His voice was low and vibrant, tinged with an underlying amusement.

Trista's eyes flew to meet his and fell away just as quickly.

'Tris?' he said softly, and the sound of her name spoken in that oddly persuasive tone set her senses singing. He took hold of her chin, turning her back to face him, and when his fingers left her skin she wanted to grasp his hand and hold it back against her.

She shook her head faintly in denial, not wanting to bring the past anywhere near this present moment, not wanting to recall what came after. This moment was going to be an incident out of time, something she could hold on to and look back on in the suddenly cold and empty years ahead. The rugged beauty of this desolate place would be forever burned in her memory as the backdrop for this afternoon with Dylan. And if she allowed the past to take over then she would have to acknowledge what he'd done.

'No. I . . . I was too young to remember much.'

His eyes searched her face. 'I remember,' he said gently. 'I can tell you anything you want to know. Your first day at school, the tricycle Ray and I painted up for you, that ragged panda you always carried around with you, the way you chattered nineteen to the dozen.'

That same electrifying tension rose again and Trista swallowed. 'You're teasing me! You couldn't possibly . . . why would you want to remember all that?' she finished unevenly.

'You were a big part of my childhood, Tris, you and Ray. I used to envy Ray having a kid sister. You were the family I didn't have.'

'But you had your own family. You had a brother.'

'Pete.' Dylan gazed back out at the ocean, his expression almost bleak. 'Pete was okay, I suppose. We were never very close. He was five years older than I was and more interested in books and geology than anything else. I guess you'd call him a loner, he always seemed happy enough with his own company.'

'He went to the United States, didn't he?'

Trista asked gently, sensing Dylan's regret over his relationship with his brother.

'Mmm. He won a scholarship to study at a university in California and then he took up a teaching post there. He was killed in a car accident in Los Angeles about eight years ago.'

'Yes, I remember that. Your father was very upset. I think he'd been expecting Pete to come home.'

Dylan nodded. 'My father thought the world of Pete.' His tone was completely expressionless. 'I guess after Pete's death he gradually lost interest in the *Blue Dancer*. I don't suppose you could blame him.'

'Have you decided what you'll do with the boat?'

'Not yet.' He sighed unconsciously. 'I may give it a go, a season or two.'

Trista picked up her mug and took another sip of her coffee. 'Have you done anything about hiring a new crew?'

'Not yet.' He shifted his weight, settling into a more comfortable position against the rocks.

His thoughts were obviously elsewhere and he made no further comment on the fishing boat, so Trista lapsed into silence. His eyes were on the incoming waves, his head turned slightly away from her so Trista could watch him unguardedly, running her eyes upwards over the long length of his jean-clad legs, the relaxed way his hands rested on his thighs, moving still higher over his flat stomach and muscular chest moulded in relief by the stiff breeze that blew the soft material of his loose sweatshirt against his body.

Her gaze slid up his arms, tanned and covered

with fine hair that was surprisingly light-coloured for one so dark. His biceps bulged and his broad shoulders she knew felt firm and smooth to the touch.

Her heart fluttered in her breast as her thoughts returned to the feel of his hard body close to hers. The wind lifted his hair, pulling it back from his forehead, and she ached to run her fingers through those dark wind-tossed strands that were short in the front and neatly shaped into the back of his neck.

If they were only two people, a man and a woman meeting in some other place, unknown to each other, discovering each other, falling in love ... Falling in love? Trista felt a swift sharp pain inside her, twisting deeply. She couldn't, mustn't, allow herself the agony of loving this man. He was Dylan Ashby, and she must always remember that.

'Do you know you still have a sprinkle of freckles across the bridge of your nose?' The sound of his voice made her start and she rubbed her finger nervously along her nose.

'Too much sun,' she said uneasily, flushing under his gaze.

His hand reached out to cover hers, lift it away from her face, but instead of releasing her he kept hold of her hand, his thumb gently rubbing the softness of her skin. The timbre of his hold changed subtly from companionable to in some not easily defined way sensual, and Trista's eyes flew upwards, to be caught once again by the depth of desire in his.

With seemingly painful slowness Dylan pulled her forward until she overbalanced and fell against him. His hands slipped up her arms to her shoulders, caressing as they went, and his lips nuzzled her temple, her cheek, the line of her jaw, until they eventually settled so exquisitely on her trembling mouth.

Trista's hands quivered against his shirt front, made one feeble effort to put some distance between them, to push herself away from the persuasion of every nuance of his hard body, the heavy mind-destroying demands of his mouth. His lips teased, tantalised, until he groaned low in his chest and his arms slid around her, binding her to him as his drugging kisses deepened.

Leaning partially across him as she was, Trista's breasts were crushed on his chest while her hands of their own accord slid around him over the soft material of his sweatshirt, feeling the hardness of his muscles underneath. His own hands played down her backbone and then slipped beneath the loose waistband of her light cotton top, setting fire to the bare skin he now touched.

His lips aroused, caressed the curve of her jaw, found the sensitive area around her ear, and she moaned softly into the hollow of his shoulder, her tonguetip tasting the tangy nectar of his skin. Her heart pounded in her ears, her senses spinning in a mad whirlpool of wanting.

Desire filled every centimetre of her throbbing body and she was convinced, could feel it was the same for him. His so obvious arousal only carried her upwards to soar higher than she had ever been before.

Dylan reversed their positions and she was lying back against the rug, his hard body leaning over her, his lips reclaiming hers in a kiss that wiped away the very last shreds of her defences. Trista arched herself closer to him and his breath seemed to catch deep in the solid wall of his chest as he whispered her name.

Lifting her, his hands slid around her, unhooking her bra, pushing the soft cotton of her top upwards to uncover her breasts, her nipples tight with her arousal. The sea breeze was cool on her heated skin and she shivered slightly as his eyes glowed with a devouring darkness.

'My God, you're so beautiful, Tris. So beautiful,' he murmured thickly as his lips lowered to seek the valley between her breasts.

Slowly sensual, his mouth slid over her skin, making her writhe with desire until she felt she couldn't bear the wonder of it a moment longer and she wound her fingers in his hair to guide his lips to a rosy peak. His tonguetip encircled her nipple and Trista arched impossibly closer to him, a cry of pure pleasure tumbling from her swollen lips.

His fingers played over the smoothness of her skin, searing where he touched, and her own fingers moved to push his shirt upwards so that she could feel the play of his taut muscles beneath her feverishly questing hands. He was as hard as a rock, the skin of his shoulders silkily smooth. Her fingers slid around to luxuriate in the matt of fine curling dark hair on his broad chest.

Dylan's body half covered hers, one long leg between hers as he moulded her contours against him, his hands running over the length of her jean-clad thigh until he groaned softly and rolled on to his back again, pulling her with him. Her naked breasts thrust against his bare chest and aroused, his hard thighs were rigid beneath hers while his fingers laced through the velvety length of her hair.

'Tris, we have to stop this,' he murmured thickly, his lips nuzzling the curve of her neck. 'You know that, don't you?'

'I don't want to stop,' she heard herself say in a voice that was as heavy with heightened passion as his had been. 'I never want . . . Oh, Dylan . . .' Her lips impassionedly sought his again and he crushed her to him.

When their lips finally broke apart they were both breathless and Dylan slowly shook his head as he held her away from him. His eyes were dark orbs as they settled on the curve of her breasts, taut with her arousal, but he made no move to bring her closer again as she so desperately wanted him to.

'Dylan?' she whispered, her eyes searching his face, partially reassured by the passion still reflected in his expression, in the burning glow in his eyes.

'Tris, this is madness,' he said unevenly.

'Why is it?'

'You must know the answer to that. Much more of this and I won't be able to stop.' His arms straightened, pushing her upright, and he sat up beside her.

'But, Dylan——' she began, her hand going tentatively to his arm.

'No, Tris.' With one lithe movement he was on his feet, standing with his back to her as he pulled down his shirt and ran his hand through his tussled hair.

Trista watched him for immeasurable seconds, her body numb now that he was apart from her, until the touch of the cool breeze on her bare skin suddenly made her realise she had made no move to cover herself. She fumbled agitatedly with her bra and then straightened her top before climbing shakily to her feet to stand looking at the tense closed lines of his body as he stood before her, back to her, hands on hips.

She wanted to reach out to him, step across and wrap her arms about his body, breathe again his clean fresh maleness, but the tension in his stance precluded that and she knew instinctively that if she did touch him there would be no going back.

But she wanted him dreadfully, wanted him to continue with his lovemaking, take her even higher, joined in the ultimate expression of love. Love—her heart beat a tattoo in her breast. At this moment she could admit she was head over heels in love with him and it was the most glorious feeling.

His hand moved to rub the tightened muscles in the back of his neck and a tiny smile lifted the corners of her mouth as her eyes drank in the whole wondrous length of him. He was everything, all she had yearned for, anticipated. It was as though she had been waiting for him all her life, waiting for him to come back . . .

A cold wave of reality wrapped around her heart and she almost flinched with the pain. In the mind-destroying heat of the earth-stopping passion he had aroused in her she had almost forgotten everything that had gone before. She cringed with self-revulsion.

Although the feelings he had just shown her she possessed were an incredible revelation to her, for him it had all happened before on heaven knew how many occasions. It had all happened before with her mother. Hadn't he touched her mother just as intimately as she had allowed him to touch her? Oh, no!

Trista turned away from him to lean weakly on the outcrop of rock they had been using for a backrest. How could she have been so foolish, so blindly naïve? How could she have forgotten? And if Dylan hadn't drawn a halt to their lovemaking she wouldn't have been capable of denying him, and that would have been the final degradation.

'Tris!' His fingers were on her arm as he turned her back to face him.

'Don't, Dylan.' Her voice squeezed thinly though her constricted throat.

'Look, I shouldn't have let that happen,' he began.

'It was as much my fault as yours,' she admitted, swallowing the lump that threatened to choke her.

'Perhaps, but I feel responsible . . .'

'I'm not a child, Dylan,' she cut him off, a tinge of bitterness in her tone.

'No, you're not that.' He smiled crookedly. 'The little freckle-faced tomboy with her hair in pigtails and those big green eyes has well and truly grown up!'

His finger traced the curve of her cheek and settled softly on her lips. Trista shivered at the renewed intimacy, her traitorous body clamouring once more for the feel of his arms locked about her. How she craved the ecstatic security she found pressed closely against him!

What type of person was she? she asked herself as she made herself step away from him, using all the willpower she could muster to drag her eyes from that same fire that burned in the dark depths of his. Her hand lifted in a feeble effort to hold him away from her.

'Don't touch me, Dylan—please!'

'That's a tall order, Tris,' he said quietly. 'The fact is I can't seem to keep my hands off you.' His hands lingered on her shoulder, trailed down her arm, his fingers twining with hers.

And she let him do it, part of her filled with self-derision, part of her exalting in his nearness. Wanting him to touch her had the upper hand no matter how much she despised herself for her weakness.

'Tris.' He murmured her name in a thick voice and lifted her hand to his lips.

The touch of his mouth was an exquisite torture and she closed her eyes tightly, swallowing the rush of tears that threatened to fall.

'I think perhaps we should move on. This place is far too isolated and far too inviting.' His thumb gently caressed the softness of her hand.

She nodded, and with obvious reluctance Dylan released her hand and bent down to shake out and refold the rug while Trista picked up the thermos and coffee mugs. Dylan made no move to take her arm as they returned to the car.

The ocean didn't seem quite so blue somehow on the drive back. They passed a couple of stalking emus picking at the stunted coastal bushes and in the distance a group of half a dozen kangaroos hopped away across the limestony paddock. Ordinarily the sight of the emus would have delighted Trista, but she made no comment, and neither did Dylan.

CHAPTER EIGHT

'My turn to offer a cup of coffee,' he said as he helped her from the car.

Trista stood beside him, drawn to him, knowing she should be sensible and flee across the road to home and safety.

'Seeing we didn't get to drink our cup out at Cape Carnot, I take the blame for that, too,' he added, a flash of that same passion flaring in his eyes.

'There's no need to go to the trouble,' she began a little breathlessly. 'I think I should go home. Besides . . .' she stopped, feeling a flush wash over her cheeks. To be alone with Dylan in the intimacy of his house would be simply asking for trouble.

'Besides?' He raised one dark eyebrow questioningly and then gave a soft velvet laugh that played a sense-searing melody on Trista's nerve-ends.

Every part of him was so blatantly, so sensually masculine that she felt as if she was on a roller-coaster soaring upwards, unable to get off but knowing eventually she would come careering downwards.

'I . . . I don't think . . .' She swallowed convulsively.

'That being alone together at the moment would be such a sensible idea,' Dylan finished. His finger trailed tantalisingly down her cheek. 'I agree with that, but we won't be alone. My aunt will make the coffee and will be a more than adequate chaperone.' He took her arm, turning her towards the house. 'Come on. My aunt will probably remember you when you had those freckles and pigtails!' He laughed again as he drew her arm through his.

'I didn't know you had an aunt in Lincoln,' Trista remarked.

'She's been back for a couple of months, staying with my uncle in Wangary. She hasn't been back in Lincoln for years either. She came to stay with us after my mother died and she remained with us until she married and moved to Murray Bridge, so I guess you could say she brought me up.'

Dylan led her up the steps into a large kitchen, much the same size as the kitchen in their house, although it hadn't had the extensive remodelling that Ray had done for Joanne in the Vaughan house. But still it had a charm all its own and looked homely and welcoming.

'Aunt Jean?' Dylan called as they walked inside and a short petite woman appeared from the hallway.

'Dylan, you're early!' She turned her smile on Trista. 'Hello there.'

'Hello,' Trista smiled.

'Aunt Jean, this is Trista Vaughan,' Dylan told her. 'Tris, Jean Parker, my father's sister.'

'Trista Vaughan? Not Ray's little sister?'

'The same,' grinned Dylan, putting his arm easily about Trista's shoulders.

'Well! I remember you when you were a baby,'

the older woman beamed. 'And how's Ray? He was only a boy when I saw him last.'

'He's fine,' Trista smiled back, knowing the colour had washed her cheeks as Dylan's arm, for all that it was a casual gesture, sent tingling sparks of awareness through her body.

'Ray and his wife are expecting their first child,' Dylan put in, 'and both looking forward to the happy event, by all accounts.'

'Yes, they certainly are,' Trista agreed, thankful that Dylan had removed his arm from her shoulder and walked across to switch on the electric kettle.

'Now, Dylan, I'll do that.' Jean Parker bustled over to take the kettle from him. 'You just take Trista through to the living room and I'll have a cuppa on in a jiffy. Or would you prefer coffee to tea, Trista?' she turned to enquire over her shoulder.

'Tea would be fine,' Trista told her.

'We'll stay here in the kitchen.' Dylan smiled at Trista and pulled a rueful face behind his aunt's back. Trista's eyes dropped to her hands as she read the message in his eyes. The living room alone would be another mistake.

Dylan pulled out a chair for Trista, but before he could seat himself the telephone jangled and he excused himself to answer it. With his departure went some of the tension that was holding Trista rigid, but perversely she yearned for him to come back. She seemed to be spinning out of control with no hold at all on her thoughts or her body's responses.

This has to stop—and now, she told herself forcefully. Nothing but pain can ever come of it.

You have to remember who he is. Remember he's Dylan Ashby. And remember what he's done, she repeated to herself, like a self-protective chant.

'Dylan tells me the *Blue Dancer* was in a terribly neglected state,' Jean Parker was saying, and Trista pulled her thoughts into order, hoping she hadn't missed anything the older woman had said.

'Yes, it was pretty bad,' she replied quickly.

'Tsk, tsk! And Bill, that's Dylan's father, used to be so particular about his boat. Such a pity!' Jean shook her head as she placed a fine lace cloth over the gleaming laminex surface of the table. 'He made fishing his life after his wife died. He had another smaller boat before the *Blue Dancer* but that was some time before the tuna fishing industry really started going ahead as it has done.'

'Did you used to live in Port Lincoln too?' asked Trista.

'Oh yes. I was born here, and so was Dylan's father and our father before us.' What were obviously the best china cups and saucers were placed on the table and Jean indicated them proudly. 'This set belonged to Dylan's grandmother, who passed it on to Dylan's mother.'

'I don't think I can remember Dylan's mother,' Trista frowned.

'Oh, no, you wouldn't. She died before you were born. She was never very strong and the doctor warned her not to have any more children after Peter, but she wanted sons for Bill. Of course, that never meant as much to Bill as she thought it did, but——' She shrugged. 'Bill's only dream in those days was to own a fleet of tuna boats. Anyway, after Dylan was born poor Ellie just didn't seem to recover. She rarely left her bed, although she lived until Dylan was about three or four.'

'Dylan said you brought him up,' Trista prompted, enjoying hearing about Dylan's family, for it was a subject that she had never heard discussed at home. No mention had ever been made of the Ashbys after——

'I suppose you could say I did raise Dylan,' Jean Parker smiled reminiscently. 'I came to help out just after he was born, when Ellie was so weak, so I guess I felt something like a mother when it came to the two boys, but especially Dylan.' She frowned momentarily. 'I know it was a terribly hard decision for me to make when my George wanted us to marry and take on the farm he bought up the river. I felt as if I was deserting the boys, but Bill insisted that they would be able to manage. He said I deserved a life of my own.'

She turned absently to switch off the kettle and pour the hot water into the silver teapot. 'I really missed the boys, but I didn't ever regret the decision. George and I had a very happy marriage until his death two years ago. I'd been living with another brother in Wangary when Dylan arrived and asked me to give him a hand with the house until he sorted everything out.'

'Do you think he'll sell the boat or work it himself?' Trista asked her softly.

'I don't know, love. He hasn't said one way or the other.' Jean shook her head a little sadly. 'That boat was always a bone of contention between Dylan and his father.'

'Why was that?' Trista asked in surprise.

'Because right from when he was a little boy Bill always talked of the time Dylan would take over the boat from him, and in the beginning Dylan went along with it. But as he grew up he tried to tell his father he wasn't interested in becoming a fisherman, and I'm afraid Bill used to insist. They always seemed to be arguing about it.'

'But what about Peter? As the older son I would have thought he would have taken over the *Blue Dancer*.'

'Oh, no, Bill never even considered Peter. Perhaps if Peter had been different——' Jean shrugged. 'You see, Peter was like his mother, tall and fairer than Dylan, and not as robust. As a child he had a weak chest and we were always doctoring his colds and 'flu. And yet, strange as it may seem,' she lowered her voice conspiratorially, 'Bill favoured Peter. I always used to think he was too hard on Dylan, expecting him to want what he wanted. I suppose Bill realised Peter would never be strong enough to take over the boat, so that left Dylan.'

'Dylan said he'd never wanted to be a fisherman,' Trista remarked reflectively.

'No, he didn't. And he was as stubborn as his father. The more Bill pushed the idea on to him the harder Dylan dug in his heels. Poor Dylan! His mother was too ill to have much time for him and his father was forever trying to make him into a reflection of himself. I don't think Dylan had a terribly happy childhood, one way and another. Perhaps that was why he was such a tearaway when he was in his teens. The things they got up to, your brother, Ray, and Dylan!' she laughed.

'Did I hear my name mentioned?' Dylan asked as he walked in to join them.

'You know what they say about eavesdroppers?' his aunt told him, and Dylan grimaced.

'Then perhaps I don't want to know what was said after all,' he smiled his thanks as his aunt passed him his coffee.

The remainder of the afternoon flew by, and it was one of the most enjoyable times Trista had had for some time. Nothing more was said on a personal note by either Dylan or his aunt, and it was with some surprise that Trista realised that the daylight that had been streaming into the comfortable old kitchen was beginning to wane.

'You're welcome to stay to dinner,' suggested Aunt Jean as she crossed to flick on the light switch. 'Isn't she, Dylan?'

'Of course,' he smiled easily.

'Oh, no, I'm sorry, I can't.' Trista stood up. 'My sister-in-law is expecting me to have dinner with them. In fact, I should be helping her with the preparation, so I must be getting along. Joanne gets rather tired easily these days. But thank you for the invitation anyway.'

'That's all right, love. You must come another time, mustn't she, Dylan?' beamed the older woman.

'She must,' Dylan agreed firmly, his eyes alight with amusement. 'I'll walk you home.' He pushed back his chair and stood up, his height and breadth dwarfing the kitchen.

'There's no need to do that. It's just across the street,' Trista protested again, moving towards the doorway.

'I insist.' He followed her, beside her in two strides. 'Won't be long, Aunt Jean.'

'Goodbye, Mrs Parker. Thank you for the cup of tea,' was all Trista had time to say as Dylan took her arm and led her outside.

They were silent as they walked over the road, but as they reached Trista's house she slowed, the now familiar tension at his nearness gripping her in its hold. 'I could easily have come across on my own,' she remarked, the tension adding a sharpness to her voice. And she was a little annoyed at the way he'd seemed to hurry her out of his house.

'You could,' he agreed softly. 'But would you have denied me this moment alone with you?' His voice vibrated close to her ear as he turned her to face him, pulling her into the circle of his arms. 'Oh, Tris,' he groaned, his lips against the curve of her throat, 'I've been longing to hold you, to kiss you again since we left Cape Carnot.'

'Dylan, we shouldn't——' Her words were lost in his mouth as his lips covered hers, and at their touch any denial she had been going to make died a very sudden death.

Her mouth opened beneath his and her hands slid around his hard back, her fingertips eagerly playing over the tautness of his muscles. She was drowning again, and she could summon not one skerrick of willpower to push him away, to break the surface of the tide that was rushing to engulf her.

Feather-soft, his lips whispered over her face, his hands cupping the back of her head, twining in her hair, fanning her senses to flame, to burn through her body. She knew she should stop him, but at that moment to make any move to end his embrace, to push him away, to halt the wondrous ecstasy of his drugging kisses, was an abject impossibility. Rather she might have attempted to stop the world from turning.

His hands moved downwards over her back to her hips, sliding over her buttocks to propel her closer to his taut thighs, making her completely conscious of his burning arousal, and she exalted in it. No man had ever stirred her, lifted her, made her so aware of her own femininity as this man did.

His teeth gently bit her earlobe and a wave of pure desire washed over her, destroying any consciousness she had of her surroundings. Had anyone so much as suggested that Trista Vaughan would have been standing here in front of her home, and that she would be locked in a man's arms without one single shred of contrition that she was in full view of anyone who cared to be passing she would have been totally horrified.

But in Dylan's arms she found that the rest of the world ceased to exist. There was only Dylan and herself, living and breathing for this moment and this moment alone.

Trista moaned low in her throat, a deeply sensual sound she barely recognised as her own voice, and her lips rained soft kisses along the line of his jaw. His skin was just slightly beard-roughened and he smelled clean and totally masculine.

'Trista,' he murmured against her mouth, his hand sliding upwards over her ribcage to cup one burgeoning breasts, his fingertips teasing her erect nipple through the thin cotton of her top. 'We have to stop this or I'll make love to you here on the grass,' he said brokenly, his voice thick with pulsating desire.

The sound of the car went unnoticed by both of them as they stood locked together lost in each other and their mutual entranced arousal, but the bright flash of the headlights that threw them into a pool of brilliant illumination had Dylan's lips drawing away from hers with a suddenness that was almost painful. His hand moved from her breast to her back, although his arms didn't surrender her from their solid safety. Had he taken his arms away Trista had no doubt that her rubbery legs would have given away beneath her.

The headlights were snapped off and the instantaneous darkness was no less blinding. Trista gulped a shaky breath, blinking to discern the dark shape that climbed from the car and closed the door with a restrained click that seemed to scream into the dusk.

Recognising the broad form as her brother, Trista pushed agitatedly against Dylan's chest, but he held her fast for what could only have been a lifetime before his grip relaxed and he allowed her to step shakily away from him. She shivered as reaction set in.

'Ray, I——' Her voice cracked and broke and she swallowed convulsively.

'What the hell do you think you're doing, Ashby?' Ray growled, ignoring his sister, his whole stance one of inflamed aggression as he faced the other man in the dimness of the soft twilight.

Beside her Dylan shifted his weight almost imperceptibly and Trista sensed that his outwardly relaxed pose only barely disguised his poised watchfulness. He was a predator prepared to defend himself against anything and anyone.

'Ray, please!' Trista appealed to her brother. 'I was just going inside. Joanne will be waiting dinner.' She took a step forwards, her hand going out to clasp his arm, her fingers feeling the tensed muscles beneath his shirt. Ray too was ready to take the whole thing further.

He shook her hand off his arm. 'Go inside, Trista. Ashby and I have some——' he paused, 'talking to do.'

'There's nothing to talk about, Ray,' Trista began.

'Trista, I told you to go inside!' Ray bit out.

'Go inside, Tris,' Dylan repeated quietly, and she gazed in disbelief from one to the other.

Surely they wouldn't—'No!' She stamped her foot. 'I won't go inside! I won't just trot off like a good little girl! I'm not leaving you two here so that you can behave like a couple of irate schoolboys!'

'Trista!' Ray took his eyes off Dylan and glared at her. 'Get the hell out of here!'

'I said I won't and I meant it.' She stood her ground. 'I'm not having you or anyone fighting over me as though I was a piece of prime steak or something!'

'I'm not letting this . . . this bloody overgrown gigolo——'

'Ray, stop it!' Trista cried out, and Dylan put a restraining hand on her arm.

'No, Tris, let him finish. Seems as if Ray wants to get something off his chest, and now's as good a time as any for him to do it.'

'It's not! It couldn't be worse. Don't you see? He's angry and——'

'Too damn right I'm angry!' Ray growled. 'Why wouldn't I be angry, arriving home to find Dylan Ashby making love to my sister in full view of the whole neighbourhood?'

'Surely that's Trista's business, and I would have thought she was old enough to make those sort of decisions for herself,' Dylan said evenly, and Trista watched Ray's hands curl into fists. 'She's not a child any longer, Ray. Maybe you should face up to that fact.'

'Dylan, please——' Trista pleaded with him. He was only making things worse.

The patio light overhead flashed on, the abruptness of it causing the three of them to glance upwards.

'Ray? What on earth are you shouting about?' Joanne peered over the railing. 'I could hear you in the kitchen! Tris?' Joanne frowned, seeing her sister-in-law. 'What's going on?'

'Nothing, Joanne.' Trista sent a warning look across at her brother. 'Dylan brought me home. He was just leaving, weren't you?' she appealed to him, and his eyes held hers for a long moment before he glanced back at Ray.

'Yes, I was just about to leave. See you some other time, Joanne. Trista.' Dylan nodded at Ray and stepped calmly around him, striding off into the now enveloping darkness.

'Tea's ready to be served.' Joanne broke the strained silence that fell with Dylan's departure. 'So come on upstairs you two.'

'I'll ... I'll just comb my hair and ... tidy up a little and I'll be right there.' Trista looked back at Ray.

'Okay. Don't be long.' Joanne walked back inside.

'Ray, please, don't make anything out of this,' Trista begged him quietly.

'Make anything out of it? You've got to be kidding! That—that embrace, for want of a better word, was downright indecent, Tris, and with someone like Dylan Ashby—God, do you know what you were inviting out here in the street? You forget, I know Dylan Ashby of old. I used to watch him in action, and believe me, he's no slouch when it comes to making out!'

'And you were so lily-white?' Trista snapped back at him, pain clutching at her heart. Hadn't she known all along that what Ray said was true and Dylan's lovemaking could hardly brand him as a novice when it came to women?

'We're not talking about me. We're talking about you and Ashby!'

'Oh, for heaven's sake, Ray! I'm well over eighteeen and legally an adult, so surely it's my business what I do, isn't it?'

'Trista, you're still my sister and I——' Ray paused, searching for words.

'You don't want your sister making a name for herself,' Trista finished, and gave a bitter laugh. 'It may interest you to know I've made a name for myself already!'

'Trista, I don't believe——'

'Well, I have. A couple, in fact. Being my mother's daughter had my name preceding me somewhat, and when they found that didn't exactly fit—well, I became known as something of a frigid little virgin. Don't you think that being branded a frigid twenty-one-year-old virgin is making a name for myself, apart from the novelty value of it in these liberated times, that is?'

Ray gazed at her open-mouthed and Trista laughed, the sound thin and high in her own ears.

'Well, it's true, Ray. Don't tell me you haven't noticed how even the crews on the boats at the wharf treat me. You must have noticed.'

'They treat you with respect because you're my sister,' Ray began.

'They treat me with amused indifference—indifference to my face and amusement behind my back, because the word gets around that I don't come across.'

'Trista, stop this!' Ray's hands decended on her shoulders and he shook her gently. 'Look, perhaps I did overreact, but——' He ran his hand through his hair.

'You *did* overreact,' she told him firmly.

'All right, all right, I overreacted—but you took me by surprise, Tris. I didn't expect to turn into the driveway and see you in a clinch!'

They stood looking at each other in the semi-circle of light from the patio above.

'And I sure as hell didn't expect to find you in Dylan Ashby's arms!'

Trista's eyes fell from the worry in her brother's expression.

'Tris, look at me.' He waited until she had raised her head. 'Did it have to be him?' he asked quietly.

'Ray, I'm sorry, believe me. I know how it must look.'

'Do you? I mean, for pity's sake, Tris, you can't be serious about him. Think about what he's done!'

Trista spun away from him. 'Don't you think I have thought about it? I've thought about it until I can just about taste it, but——'

'Are you in love with him?'

'In love?' Trista took a steadying breath, glad he couldn't see her face. 'In love with Dylan Ashby? Don't be silly, Ray!' It took every ounce of her willpower to give a laugh that passed for disdainful amusement. 'He's simply a very attractive man and he was—well,' she shrugged her shoulders, 'he was there. And maybe I was looking for a bit of experience. That's all.'

'Trista.' Ray reached out to put his hand on her arm, but she moved away from him. 'Sis, I don't want you to get hurt.'

'I know, Ray,' she said wearily. 'We'd better go inside or Joanne's dinner will be ruined.'

CHAPTER NINE

To say that their family meal that evening had not been successful after her argument with Ray was't strictly true. Both Joanne and Trista made a light effort at conversation and at times so did Ray, but quite often throughout the meal Trista found Ray's eyes on her, and his expression was troubled.

At the beginning of the meal Joanne made tentative enquiries about Trista's afternoon with Dylan, but Trista managed to sidetrack her questions, turning the discussion to babies' names, and Joanne was only too eager to talk about the subject closest to her heart. However, Trista knew she hadn't heard the end of it from Joanne. Her sister-in-law couldn't help but have noticed the ill-feeling that had emanated from Ray towards Dylan, and she wondered how much Ray would have told his wife after Trista had left them.

She tossed and turned in bed for hours trying to wash out the memory of Dylan's lovemaking, but as she lay there alone she could almost feel the touch of his hands and his lips and her body burned, craving an unknown satisfaction that she knew instinctively Dylan would have assuaged had she surrendered completely to him.

And she would have surrendered to him totally, without reservation, for she realised she had been away beyond the point of no return. Dylan couldn't help but have known she was, too, and yet he hadn't taken advantage of her.

She writhed on her dishevelled bed, her thoughts ricocheting around in her head. Why hadn't he? That he found her attractive, was as aroused as she had been, he had been unable to hide. In fact, he hadn't tried to disguise it. So why had he been the one to call a halt to their lovemaking? Unless it was the very same reason he had turned away from her before—she reminded him of her mother.

That thought made her sick with self-loathing and she wrapped her arms about her body in some deference to the pain that racked her to her very soul. Her heart ached with a pain that became almost unbearable. What was she to do? She'd have to make a decision about this, and quickly, before the situation got even more out of hand.

It would be for the best if she stopped it now, she could see that. The more she saw of Dylan the more involved she became. She forced aside the thought that it was too late, that she was in over her head already.

And *his* motives? If they were purely physical why hadn't he pressed his advantage? When he touched her he couldn't help but know that he had the upper hand, that she was his for the taking.

Trista groaned into her pillow. Had she no pride? No self-respect? Could she have fallen so completely in love with him, knowing of his previous involvement with her mother?

A teardrop spilled over her cheek and she dashed it away with an irascible hand. This bout of self-pity wasn't going to help at all, she admonished herself. She would just have to keep

well away from Dylan Ashby, and having made the
decision she would have to stick to it faithfully.

But what if he should remain in Port Lincoln,
make his home here again? She'd have to see
him—he lived opposite her, when all was said and
done. Their paths were bound to cross.

The tears began to fall in earnest and she sat
up, switching on the bedside lamp and climbing
out of bed. She padded across to the bathroom
and washed her flushed face. Her eyes reflected
in the mirror looked large and bright with unshed
tears, and a terrible sadness gripped her. Leaning
against the vanity unit, she began to shake with
sobs and she knew she was crying because she
would somehow be losing something immensely
precious, for Dylan Ashby had become very
special to her. And she cried because she knew
she would have to make the break with him. She
wouldn't be able to face herself if she didn't.

And the pain of that loss went far deeper than
any she had known before. It was an agony more
terrible than a child's loss of her mother.

Trista overslept the next morning and after
rushing about getting ready for work she was
halfway to the office before she realised it was
Trent's birthday and that she had left the gift she
had bought him at home. By the time she'd
returned home, collected the birthday present
and driven back to work she was ten minutes late.

Hurrying into her office, she reached out
automatically to switch on the coffee machine on
her way to the door to Trent's office. She gave a
quick knock and opened the door, breathing a
sigh of relief when she saw that the office was
empty. Slipping inside, she set the small gift-

wrapped box on his desk, returning to her own office just as he arrived.

'Morning, Trista,' he smiled at her. 'I'm afraid I slept in this morning.'

'I did too. Happy birthday, by the way.' She sat down at her desk.

'Thanks. Thirty-five seems something of a milestone somehow.' He grinned. 'I may stay at thirty-five now I've reached it! Thirty-five always sounds old enough but not too old.'

He went through to his office and returned a moment later with the cufflinks she had given him.

'Tris! They're lovely. Thanks very much,' he beamed at her.

'That's okay. I'm glad you like them.'

'I do.' He went to turn away, his fair skin slightly tinged with pink. 'Trista?'

She glanced up at him.

'How about having dinner with me tonight?'

'Oh, I don't . . .'

He held up his hand. 'Don't refuse. No one should spend their thirty-fifth birthday dining alone, should they?'

Trista wavered. Until now she had always made a point of refusing Trent's invitations, but surely if the intentions of her sleepless night before were to be upheld then what better start than to accept Trent's offer of dinner? As he said, it was his birthday and he shouldn't have to spend the evening alone.

'Well——' she paused. 'I . . . that would be nice.'

His face broke into a a huge smile that touched her slightly guilty conscience. 'Great! How would seven-thirty suit you?'

'Fine.'

'Great!' Trent repeated, all but glowing as he disappeared into his office.

As he left a sinking feeling of regret immediately assailed her, adding to her guilt. She should have refused him. Feeling the way she did about Dylan she was hardly being fair on Trent, and he didn't deserve to be used in any way.

But she wasn't using him exactly, she told herself. He did want company on his birthday and she would simply be sharing a meal with him, but ... She felt so callous somehow. She should go in to him and tell him the truth, explain. But how could she explain without revealing too much?

Damn Dylan Ashby! He was the cause of all this. Life had seemed so even-flowing until he turned up. She had had everything in perspective, had built a very safe little barrier about herself and she had been happy living her life within it. Dylan Ashby had broken through that wall and she was now more vulnerable than she had ever been.

Well, she must simply keep clear of Dylan Ashby, that was all. She had made the decision and if nothing else her dinner with Trent was at least a step in the right direction.

Reaching across, she switched on the answering machine and rewound the tape. She jotted down the first message to pass on to Trent.

'Tris.' The sound of his deep voice coming out of the answering machine caught her like a blow to the solar plexus and her numbed brain just didn't compute the remainder of the message. With shaky hands she rewound it and listened with impatience to a repeat of the first message before his voice said her name again with that same low intimacy.

'Tris, thanks for the afternoon yesterday. I enjoyed it.' There was a pause. 'We need to talk. Have dinner with me tonight. I'll pick you up around seven o'clock and we'll go somewhere quiet, I'll leave the choice of the place up to you. And tell Trent I'll be in to see him about nine this morning.'

His voice stopped and the silence whirred on. Trista sat and gazed at the machine.

'But I can't,' she spoke out loud, and the sound of her own voice brought her out of her shocked immobility.

And she'd told Trent she'd dine with him. How she wished she hadn't! Why had it to be tonight? This particular night of all nights.

The thought of a secluded dinner with Dylan, just the two of them, had her heart pounding in her breast. No! She covered her face with her hands. Where was her decisiveness now? No, in no circumstances must she allow herself to be alone with Dylan Ashby.

She would just have to phone him and tell him she was sorry but that she had a previous engagement. And it was the truth, too! A cold despair clutched at her and when the intercom buzzed she literally jumped with fright.

'Yes, Trent?'

'Any messages?' he asked.

'Oh, yes. Sorry—I was just going to bring them in.' She pulled herself together with no little effort. 'Mr Partridge called. He'll be away until Friday, and,' she gulped a breath, 'Dylan Ashby said he would see you this morning at nine.'

'It's about that now, isn't it?'

Trista glanced at her watch. 'Yes.'

'Well, send him straight in when he arrives. Oh, and how about some coffee?' he added.

'How about a cup for me, too?' said a deep voice at her elbow.

She spun around and her heart lurched heavily in her breast, taking her breath away. She hadn't heard him come in, and to turn and find him standing there was almost more than she could bear. He was leaning nonchalantly against the corner of her desk and he was so vitally attractive that she was unable to find her voice.

His light-coloured safari suit hugged his broad shoulders and the contrasting autumn-toned fine striped shirt accentuated the darkness of his eyes, the blackness of his hair. He was by far the most assertively masculine man she had ever seen.

She wanted to obey the dictates of her heart, to fly around the desk to him, to touch him, feel his arms about her again, to know the pressure of his lips on hers again. Fool! she cried at herself. You're a fool, Trista Vaughan. You made a decision last night, no one coerced you into making it, so have the guts to stick to it. No good can come of any relationship you would have with Dylan Ashby. In no time he'll be gone.

'Good morning,' she got out at last. 'You can go straight in.' She turned to the coffee-maker to set out two mugs.

Strong arms encircled her from behind, propelled her back against his hard length, and the breath left her body in a startled gasp.

'Tris,' he murmured into the curve of her neck, 'I spent the most frustrating, sleepless hours of my life last night.' His breath fanned her ear, sending slivers of desire to pierce her heart. 'I've been longing to get you back into my arms.' He lowered his voice. 'I don't suppose you had trouble sleeping, too, did you?'

'Dylan, please!' She tried to pry his fingers from the flatness of her midriff.

'Mmm, you smell divine. What is that perfume?' His lips nuzzled her earlobe and she felt her legs go to water beneath her.

'Dylan, stop it! I'm supposed to be working, and Trent,' she gulped a steadying breath, 'Trent wouldn't like it.'

His arms slowly released her. 'No, I guess it's not the time or the place, but I sure enjoyed it.' His laugh was low in his throat and vibrated through her, making her want to turn back into his arms, renew the exquisite feeling of having their strength about her.

'God, Tris, don't look at me like that or I won't be responsible for my actions,' he said thickly, and her senses tingled at the leashed passion in his voice. He ran a hand through his hair and sighed, smiling crookedly. 'I think I'd better go in and see your boss.'

He moved towards the door, stopping with his hand on the doorknob. 'Until tonight,' he said, his tone a promise, as he knocked on the wooden panel and went inside.

Trista raised her hand to call him back, but the door had closed behind him before she found her voice and she groaned softly. Tonight. She had to tell him there wouldn't be a 'tonight'. There must never be one. Tears sprang to her eyes again and she blinked them back. She had to remain firm.

She poured the coffee with a shaky hand and taking a deep breath followed Dylan through to Trent's office.

'Ah, coffee!' Trent smiled. 'I can't start the day properly without it and I was running too late to have a cup before I left home this morning.' He sipped the steaming black liquid with relish. 'Thanks, Trista, you're a lifesaver, besides being the best secretary in Port Lincoln.'

Flushing, Trista turned to pass Dylan his cup and he smiled his thanks, his eyes moving over her, lazily provocative, sending a message that fired her blood.

'How about this for a nice pair of cufflinks!' Trent's voice cut between them and he held out the box to show Dylan. 'Trista has good taste, doesn't she?' he beamed at her.

'Yes, she has,' Dylan replied easily, his eyes on her lips.

'It's a birthday gift,' Trent expanded. 'I'll wear them tonight when we go out to dinner, Tris,' he added, happily unaware of the sudden tenseness his words created.

Trista watched the change in Dylan's stance, saw him straighten, his body flexed as his eyes snapped back to her face. The burning glow in his eyes was shielded now by his partially lowered lids and his jaw had a set tightness about it.

Her heart sank to bedrock. Why had Trent had to say that? She'd wanted to tell Dylan herself. She owed him that.

'Dylan tells me his boat's well on the way to being back to its best,' Trent was saying, and Trista nodded dully.

'That's good news,' she remarked flatly, knowing she had to escape from the coolness in Dylan's expression. 'Well, I'll get back to work.' She turned quickly and had to stop herself running to the door and the relative sanctuary of her own office.

She sank down on to her chair. She'd have to explain when he came out, tell him the arrangements had been made before she'd turned on the answering machine. Her heart felt like lead and she glanced across at the door, willing Dylan to come out so that she could put the explanation behind her.

Ten minutes later he hadn't appeared, so she tried to immerse herself in her work, but no matter how hard she tried the heaviness sat on her, her nerve ends tightening to screaming pitch as she waited for Dylan to leave Trent's office.

When the door eventually did open she jumped like a startled fawn, her fingers jerking uselessly on the wrong typewriter keys.

'I'll come down and have a look at the boat myself in a day or two,' Trent was saying as he walked across to the outer door with Dylan. 'And just give me a buzz if I can be of any assistance in the meantime.'

'Thanks.' Dylan's eyes went momentarily to Trista, meeting hers with a coldness that chilled her, reaching down to her soul. And he left without a word.

Trista wanted to telephone him, but each time she calmed her pulsating senses and reached for the phone to call his home no one answered. The entire afternoon she spent in court with Trent and by five o'clock it was all she could do to drag herself home, sick at heart at the thought of the evening ahead. And Trent's parting words, 'Until tonight,' hadn't helped a bit. They simply brought the sound of Dylan's voice back to her to taunt her.

She lay in a warm scented bath trying to soothe her tensed muscles, but she was just as tired, as dispirited as she towelled herself dry half an hour later. She knew she had to ring Dylan, and deciding there was no putting it off a moment longer she wrapped herself in her bathsheet and crossed determinedly to the telephone.

Jean Parker answered.

'This is Trista Vaughan here, Mrs Parker. Is Dylan there?' she asked breathily.

'No, love, he hasn't arrived home yet. I think he's down at the boat. Can I give him a message or get him to phone you when he gets in?'

'No. No, thanks. I'll try again tomorrow. 'Bye for now.' She slowly replaced the receiver and walked back into the bedroom feeling frustrated and close to tears.

Slowly she began to dress. She glanced without interest at the clothes hanging in her wardrobe, flicking over the soft green crêpe she had worn to Tom and Maree's wedding. Had it only been two days ago? So much seemed to have happened since then. It would have been a form of blissful torture to slip the soft folds over her head.

Angrily she cast the dress aside and chose a cool cream smock of soft cheesecloth and hand-crocheted lace. As she walked back into the living-room her eyes were drawn to the paintings of Whaler's Way and she could almost feel again the hardness of Dylan's body pressed against hers as they lay together on the rug, the ocean crashing on the rocks below them.

She gave herself a mental shake and forced all thoughts of Dylan to the back of her mind. At least she tried to. Glancing at her wristwatch, she walked outside and up the back stairs to see Joanne.

'Hi, Joanne! Anyone home?' she called at the open door of the kitchen.

'In the bedroom, Tris,' came Joanne's muffled voice, and Trista hurried through to the front of the house.

'Joanne, what's wrong? Aren't you feeling well?' she frowned, disturbed by her sister-in-law's pale face.

'I'm fine now,' Joanne assured her, propping herself up against her pillows. 'I must have eaten something that didn't go down too well with Junior,' she grimaced, 'and I felt a little off colour.' She flexed her back stiffly.

'Oh, Joanne! Will Ray be back tonight?'

'Probably not. He's taken the *Shelly Star* out. I was fine when he left.'

'Have you had some dinner? Do you want me to get you anything?' asked Trista, still not convinced that Joanne was feeling better.

'No, thanks, love. As I didn't have to cook a big meal for Ray I just had a snack, and I've been relaxing like the lady of the manor ever since,' Joanne grinned.

Trista sat down on the edge of the bed. 'You still look a bit pale. Are you sure you don't want me to call the doctor just to be on the safe side?'

'No. Honestly, Tris, I've felt much better since I lay down. I'll get up soon and have a nice shower and then an early night.'

'Are you sure you had enough to eat? I could make you an omelette in no time,' Trista suggested.

'No, thanks. I managed a sandwich and I had a cuppa. I'll be okay now.'

'Maybe I should stay with you,' Trista began.

'Don't be silly, love, you're not spoiling your night out. Where are you off to anyway?'

'It's Trent's birthday and he didn't want to have dinner on his own, so I agreed to go with him.'

'Trent?' Joanne raised her eyebrows. 'But I thought you weren't keen on that idea.'

'I wasn't—I'm not.' Trista stood up and paced about the room. 'But I——' She shrugged. 'I could hardly refuse, as it was his birthday. Anyway, it's only a meal. I'll be home early as we've had a hard day and I'm sure Trent won't want to make it too late a night either. I know I'm tired before I start. It's been ages since we've had such a hectic day.'

'Where's he taking you?' Joanne shifted gingerly on her pillows.

'I don't know.' Trista smiled. 'I'm afraid the town's not littered with fancy restaurants.'

'No, you couldn't say that,' Joanne laughingly agreed. 'But we all still love the old place.' She sobered, a tiny frown creasing her forehead. 'Tris, I've been meaning to ask you. About last night——' she began, only to be interrupted by the sound of a car drawing to a halt in the driveway.

Trista walked over to the window as Trent climbed out of his BMW. 'Trent's here,' she told Joanne with some relief. Joanne would have to shelve her questions about Dylan and Ray and their brief altercation the evening before. Her eyes lifted to glance at the house across the street and in the pale moonlight she could see that Dylan's car was still not parked in the driveway.

'I'll have to go, Joanne.' Trista looked down at her sister-in-law. 'Now you're sure you'll be all right and that you don't want me to stay with you?'

'Tris, go and enjoy yourself. The telephone's right there in the kitchen and if I feel any worse I'll ring Dr Rivers, I promise. Okay?'

Trista smiled. 'All right. I won't be late anyway, so if your light's still on I'll come up and make you a cup of tea.'

'That'll be lovely.' Joanne reached out and squeezed her arm. 'Now off you go and have fun.'

'Trent! I'm upstairs!' Trista called as she closed Joanne's kitchen door and hurried down the steps. 'I'll just lock up the flat and I'll be ready.' She flicked off the lights and turned the key in the lock. 'Right. Shall we go?'

They walked out to the car and Trent opened the passenger side door for her just as a car rounded the corner, its headlights flashing over them before it swung into the driveway across the street.

'That was Dylan's Mazda, was't it?' Trent asked.

'Yes, I think so.' Trista turned to climb into the car.

'I'd forgotten he lived across from you.' Trent walked around to the driver's side and climbed behind the wheel. 'I suppose you knew him before he left Port Lincoln, then?'

'He was a school friend of Ray's,' she said. 'Where are we going?' she changed the subject quickly, not wanting to so much as think about Dylan, let alone discuss him.

CHAPTER TEN

'THAT wasn't at all bad, was it?' Trent took a sip of the coffee that rounded off their dinner.

'No. It was very nice,' Trista agreed, and she admitted to herself that she had enjoyed the meal and Trent's undemanding company.

They had talked easily about work and Trent had even told her a little about his childhood spent in Sydney and then Adelaide. She had worked with him for four years and yet she realised she knew very little about him. His parents, he told her, were retired and lived outside Adelaide, and he had two sisters, both married, who also lived in Adelaide and were prone to matchmaking without any success to date.

Trent had laughed, his eyes holding that same message and Trista had shifted uneasily on her seat. She changed the subject quickly and knew he was aware that she had done so.

When they had finished their meal they left the dining room and walked through to the lounge, sitting down at a table back from the small dance floor. A five-piece band was playing and a number of couples were dancing to the music. After seeing her seated Trent walked over to the bar to order their drinks.

Trista glanced down at her wristwatch and groaned inwardly, wishing Trent had suggested they call it a night when they finished their meal.

Her head had started aching slightly and she had to stifle a yawn. Trent started back with the drinks and she gave him a faint smile.

Her line of vision skipped past him to a table across the room to his right as a strident female laugh drew her attention. Trista recognised Gay Richards immediately. She sat with a grey-haired man Trista knew to be her boss, another younger man Trista didn't know—and her eyes widened as they took in the fourth person seated at the table. Dylan sat side on to her, his dark head in profile, and to all outward appearances he was thoroughly enjoying himself, smiling with the other two men at Gay's remark.

A sharp pain clutched at her heart. He hadn't wasted much time finding a substitute for tonight, she thought wryly. At that moment Gay caught sight of Trista and her eyebrows rose, her hand reaching out to touch Dylan's arm.

Dylan turned slowly, his eyes settling on Trista and then Trent for long moments before his lips lifted in a cynical smile and he turned back to Gay, leaning closer to her to make some remark that she found hilarious. Trista felt physically ill. She wished she could get up and escape to the sanctuary of home, away from Dylan, away from Gay Richards, away from everything.

'Yes. Sorry, Trent, I was miles away, thinking of something else.' Her hand closed around the frosty glass of orange juice Trent had set down in front of her and she raised it to her lips. 'What were you saying?' she asked him guiltily as she replaced the glass on the table.

'Just wondered if you'd care to dance,' he repeated goodnaturedly.

'Yes, I'd like to, thanks.' Anything to shift her from the full view of that other table.

Standing up, they joined the other couples on the dance floor. Trent danced well if somewhat stiffly and Trista followed him automatically, her mind swinging back to Dylan, while she forced herself with no little effort not to even glance across at that table.

Of course, sitting out between dances it was almost impossible to block the table from her sight, and Trista's nerves tensed to fever pitch. Gay's boss and the other man left and Dylan and Gay stood up to dance. Trista turned away, smiling across at Trent, remarking on the enjoyable music, and he beamed happily at her.

'Care to dance again?'

'No!' The word burst from her. 'No,' she repeated with a little less force. 'I'd rather just sit here and listen to the music for a while, if you don't mind.'

'Of course. To tell you the truth, I'm not terribly fond of dancing. I have to concentrate too hard on keeping time.' He laughed. 'I haven't got a musical bone in my body, I'm afraid.'

'Well, hello, you two.' Gay's voice had Trista turning around with a start. 'Fancy seeing you here! What's the special occasion?'

'Only my birthday,' Trent replied, standing up. 'A very enjoyable birthday, though, I must add.' He smiled down at Trista.

Her eyes flew to Dylan and his mouth was set tautly.

'We're just here for a few drinks and a dance ourselves.' Her laughter rasped Trista's nerve ends like coarse-grained sandpaper. 'No special

event, unless you'd like to call it old times' sake.'
She smiled silkily up at Dylan as she stood close to
him, one elbow resting on his shoulder, her fingers
under her chin red-tipped nails and matching
lipstick glaring, seeming to taunt Trista.

'Have you two met, by the way?' Dylan spoke
for the first time, addressing Trent, and Gay
laughed again.

'Of course. Trent and I have known each other
for ages, haven't we?'

Trista's eyebrows rose slightly in surprise and
she turned to gaze at Trent. She wouldn't have
thought Gay was Trent's type at all.

'We met at the Rotary meetings,' Trent
explained quickly, his skin a little pink with
embarrassment. 'Would you both care to join
us?' he added, and Dylan moved towards the
chair on Trista's right, holding it out for Gay.

'Thanks.' His tone was flat and somewhat curt.

A faint frown crossed Gay's face, as though she
wasn't keen on the development, but she could
only slip into the seat Dylan held for her. He then
walked behind Trista and sat down in the seat
beside her.

Trista's mouth went completely dry as her
nerve ends tingled at his nearness and she clasped
her hands together in her lap to still their
tremble. Dylan moved slightly and his jean-clad
leg brushed hers. Trista froze in her seat, unable
to move. He shifted again and the coarse denim
caught at the soft cheesecloth of her dress.

Her eyes slid sideways to meet his, saw the
cruel amusement in their dark depths. He was
doing it on purpose, trying to get to her, and he
was succeeding. Her skin burned where he

touched her, aroused her, and he was provoking
her with cold calculation.

She shifted her position and he did likewise.
He wouldn't allow her to escape him and there
was nothing she could do about it unless she
made a scene, and she couldn't have borne that.

'Trista, aren't you in a dream tonight?' Gay's
sharp voice brought her back to the present with
a wrench. 'Trent, you must have bewitched the
girl!' she laughed.

'I'm sorry, Gay. What was it you said?' Trista
apologised.

'I just asked how Joanne was. I heard she
hasn't been having a very good time of it,' Gay
repeated exasperatedly.

'She's been quite well lately, although she
was a little off colour this afternoon,' Trista
told her.

'When's the baby due?'

'Six or seven weeks, I think. She'll be pleased
when it's all over.'

'I'll bet she will. They've been trying for a
family for so long it will be a pity of anything
goes wrong,' Gay remarked lightly.

A frown shadowed Trista's brow as she met
Gay's eyes. It was all just chat to the other girl.
She couldn't really give a damn for Joanne and
Ray, she was far too wrapped up in herself to care
about anyone else. Couldn't Dylan see how
shallow Gay's personality was?

Dylan's leg moved away from hers as he
beckoned to a passing waiter, ordering drinks for
himself and Gay after ascertaining that Trista
and Trent weren't ready for another. When the
waiter returned Dylan downed his drink in

double quick time, and Trista couldn't stop her eyes going from the empty glass back to his face.

His own eyes met hers coldly before he excused himself and strode across to the bar for a refill. If he intended drinking himself into oblivion then she didn't want to be here to see it. She put her hand to her mouth, feigning a yawn.

'Excuse me. I think our busy day has caught up with me.' She glanced across at Trent. 'Would you mind if we called it a night?'

'Of course not.' Trent stood up immediately. 'Would you excuse us?'

Dylan gave a barely discernible nod while Gay could hardly hide her pleasure at having Dylan to herself again. It suited her down to the ground. Well, Gay was welcome to him, Trista told herself as she followed Trent to the car. And it would serve her right if he did over-indulge and she had to drive him home, she thought rather bitchily.

Trent stopped the car and switched off the engine. 'Thanks for coming, Trista. This evening was just great—the best birthday I've ever had. I hope you enjoyed it as much as I did.'

'I did enjoy it,' she replied, making a big thing of searching in her bag for her key. 'Well, I guess I'll see you in the morning,' she laughed nervously, and glanced at her watch in the dim light from the dashboard. 'I'll aim to be on time if not bright and wide awake!'

'You can be late if you like, Tris,' he said softly. 'We should have a quieter day tomorrow.'

'Oh, I'll be on time,' she assured him. 'Well, goodnight, Trent, and thanks again.'

'Trista?' He put his hand on her arm. 'May I kiss you goodnight?'

His question threw her into some confusion. Had he simply leaned across and kissed her she would most probably have bolted, but his softly spoken query put the ball right back into her court and she didn't quite know how to handle it.

Perversely she thought of Dylan. If it had been Dylan sitting here beside her in the car she knew he wouldn't have asked. He would have pulled her into his arms, kissed her until she was soaring high above the ordinary plane of life. And she would have met him halfway, more than halfway. No, Dylan Ashby wouldn't have to ask.

But Trent wasn't Dylan, could never be him, and for that she should be grateful. She had to forget Dylan and his drugging kisses, wipe away the memory of his earth-shattering lovemaking, and she might as well make a start right here and now. Kissing Trent goodnight would be another step in the right direction. Away from Dylan Ashby.

'Trista?' Trent repeated.

'I . . . I think I'd like that, Trent.'

His hand took hold of hers and he leant across to put his lips tentatively on her mouth. Trista could feel herself freezing up inside. It wasn't that Trent's kisses were unpleasant—far from it. His lips were cool and gentle and his hands moved to her shoulders as he pulled her reverently into his arms.

But she was freezing up, her body crying out for other lips, other hands, another body pressed closely to hers. Panic rose inside her. What was happening to her? What had Dylan Ashby done to her? Would no other man be able to erase the memories she had stored up inside her? It was as though he had been impressed on her, a sketch in indelible ink, a painting in colour-fast oils, and no one, not Trent Hardie, no one would be able to wipe away his image.

Trista pushed agitatedly against Trent's chest and he released her. 'I'm sorry, I ...' she whispered, her voice catching in her throat. 'I ...'

'Trista, I understand. I'd be the last person to rush you.' He squeezed her hand. 'Just know that I care about you, and if you could see your way to come out with me again we could get to know each other better and——'

'No, please! Trent, don't say any more.' Guilt burned inside her. 'I don't deserve——' she stopped a lump in her throat.

'There's someone else, isn't there?' he asked without rancour.

'Don't ask me that,' she said huskily, and he gave a light laugh.

'I tried to tell myself I was mistaken at the hotel tonight when I saw the way you looked at Dylan Ashby, but I was right, wasn't I? It's him.'

Trista couldn't answer him. How she wished she was able to deny it, but somehow the words stuck in her throat and she couldn't utter them.

'Does he feel the same way?' he asked.

'Oh, Trent!' She raised her hands and let them fall.

'He must do, I guess,' he answered for her. 'That's why I was on the receiving end of some pretty fierce looks in the short time we spent with them. So if you both feel the same way where's the stumbling block?'

'There's no stumbling block the way you

mean. We just ... It wouldn't work out, that's all.'

When Trent went to comment she held up her hand. 'No, don't say any more. I'd really rather not talk about it.' She sighed. 'I did enjoy our evening, Trent. Thanks for taking me. I'm sorry about—well, about everything else.'

'There's no need to apologise.' He climbed out of the car and walked around to open her door for her. 'And I still enjoyed the evening.' He walked back and slid behind the wheel. 'See you in the morning.'

'Yes. Goodnight.' She stood watching as he backed out of the driveway and moved off down the street. She remained standing there and her eyes were drawn to the house across the road.

A light burned in a window at the back of the house, probably the kitchen, but the moon had disappeared behind some clouds and she was unable to see if Dylan's car had returned while she was talking to Trent. Some chance! she told herself angrily. He would still be enjoying himself with Gay. Why wouldn't he be? After all, Gay was giving him the most blatant green light Trista had ever seen.

She swallowed the sudden rush of tears and turned angrily away. Dylan Ashby was none of her business. He could do what he liked as far as she was concerned.

She glanced up at the house as she walked towards her flat. Joanne's light was out, so she must be asleep. Feeling for the lock, she turned the key and swung the door open. She walked desultorily through to the living-room and dropped her evening bag on to the coffee table.

The paintings mocked her from the walls as she stood before them. Well, she'd had her afternoon at Whaler's Way with Dylan and now it was over. She had to learn to live with that. Cold pain gripped her to her very soul.

The soft rap on the kitchen door made her jump with fright and it had to be repeated before she could move.

'Who is it?' she asked apprehensively, her hand on the doorknob.

'Dylan,' came the curt reply.

CHAPTER ELEVEN

'It's late. I'm tired and I was just going to bed,' she said breathily. What could he want?

'Trista, open up! We need to talk.'

'There's nothing to talk about.' Her fingers tightened on the doorknob until her knuckles turned white

'Tris, either you open the door or I'm going to break it in, so take your pick.'

'You'll . . . you'll wake everyone up.'

'At the moment I don't particularly care if the whole world gets a disturbed night,' he bit out. 'So, do I come in quietly?'

Trista slowly opened the door. He was standing in the pool of light that escaped through the doorway, aggression in every line of his body, feet set contentiously apart, hands resting firmly on his hips.

'Dylan, it's far too late——' Trista began.

Ignoring her plea, he strode past her into the kitchen and she remained by the open door holding on to it in case her shaky legs gave way beneath her.

'Hardie didn't stay long,' he remarked, his tone an insinuation.

'No, he didn't,' she agreed softly, not rising to the provocation.

'Poor chump. Does he take any little crumb you offer him?'

'Look, Dylan, I'm too tired to swap insults

with you.' She raised her chin. 'Trent and I simply went to dinner, danced, and he dropped me home,' she finished with as much disdain as she could muster.

Dylan gave a harsh laugh. 'And a chaste peck in the confines of his car.'

A dull flush washed her cheeks. 'I would have thought you might have lingered over dropping Gay home rather than hurrying back here to spy on Trent and me like some avid Peeping Tom!'

He took a step towards her, his mouth a thin line, and Trista shrank instinctively backwards. Dylan swore under his breath and raked a hand through his hair.

'You'd do well not to bait me, Tris. Not tonight. Because I'm just about ready to give you what you're asking for!'

'Asking for? I wouldn't ask you for anything, Dylan Ashby, so you may as well leave right now. I can't see that we're accomplishing anything at all, and I want to get to bed.'

'Oh, so do I, believe me. So do I.' His laugh was deep, part self-derision, part pure arousal. 'Then maybe I might get some peace,' he muttered as his hands reached out for her, drawing her against him with a force that very nearly knocked the breath from her body.

His lips took savage possession of hers, plundering, using all his male strength to force her into submission. He was the total dominant male and Trista's struggles were futile things against him. She could only let him kiss her, and a flood of tears sprang to her eyes and overflowed to course down her cheeks. She moaned softly in protest and the sound must have reached him, for his hold on her slackened, his hands now arousing rather than subjugating as they slid over her back, his lips persuasive instead of punishing, and Trista felt herself melt acquiescently against him.

When he finally raised his head he was breathing raggedly and he gazed down at her through eyes that were shielded by his lowered lashes. 'What does Trent Hardie mean to you?' he asked thickly.

'He's my boss, a friend, nothing more,' she answered him honestly, her eyes not wavering from his. His kiss had shaken her to the core and she had no thought of fabrication.

He expelled the tight breath he had been holding and some of the tension left him.

'I'd already agreed to have dinner with him to celebrate his birthday before I switched on the answering machine and—well, you arrived at the office before I had a chance to phone you and explain.'

He nodded. 'Do you realise what hell I've been through today, tonight, imagining you and Trent?' he asked her quietly. 'I had special plans for this evening.' His eyes went to her swollen lips, bruised by his harsh assault, and the pads of his thumbs gently massaged the red marks on her arms where his fingers had bitten into her skin.

'I'm sorry I hurt you, Trista. God knows I didn't mean to do it.' He released her and turned away to pace restlessly about the kitchen. 'I want you to marry me,' he said flatly.

Trista stared at him. 'Marry you?' she breathed, and for one ecstatic moment her heart soared like an eagle and for that exquisite moment she was alive with wonder. One glorious moment before it all came back to her.

'No!' The word escaped in an explosive rush and Dylan turned back to her, his face pale in the artificial light. 'No,' she repeated.

He stood watching her for immeasurable minutes before he spoke. 'Why?' he asked with cool flatness.

'Because I can't. I can't!' Her voice rose to border on hysteria and she gulped a steadying breath. 'I can't marry *you*,' she emphasised.

'You just can't? Don't I deserve an explanation? I mean—thank you, but I don't care for the colour of your hair,' he quipped sarcastically.

'You should know why I can't, Dylan.' A lump of despair rose in her chest and lodged painfully in her throat.

'I'm not a mind-reader, Trista. How the hell could I even begin to guess? All I know is you're not indifferent to me. I only have to touch you to prove that.'

Trista shook her head. 'Can't you imagine how it would look if I married you? What everyone would say?' She threw at him. 'Oh, not to our faces, but the snide remarks would follow us wherever we went.'

'What in God's name has it got to do with anyone but ourselves? I couldn't care less what people think or what they say.'

'No, I suppose you don't. You didn't before. But I do.' Her anger rose inside her like bile.

'And what exactly are these supposed people going to be saying?' His lips twisted. 'You might as well tell me the worst.'

'You can ask that even after you . . .? Dylan,

you even said I remind you of her.' The pain gripped her again and she wanted to lash out at him.

He took a couple of steps towards her. 'What on earth are you talking about?'

'My mother!' she almost yelled at him. 'That's who. The divine Angela. You said I reminded you of her, and I couldn't bear that, Dylan. Don't you see? I'd always wonder if it was me you were ...' Her voice broke on a sob and his hands reached out for her again.

'Trista, I've never said you were like your mother,' he said evenly. 'I wouldn't say you were anything like her, what I can remember of her, that is.'

'What you can remember of her?' Trista stared up at him in disbelief. 'Oh, Dylan, how could you say that so easily? She ruined her life for you!'

His eyes seemed to bore down on her, but she stood her ground.

'Well, can you deny it? Didn't you just run off with her without a thought for the family you were breaking up?'

She could almost believe that he was overcome by shock, for he made no attempt to speak until she moved out of his unresisting hold.

'Trista!' His voice was tinged with disbelief. 'Trista, I swear I——'

Whatever he was about to say was interrupted as a loud thud, like a piece of falling furniture, came from overhead. They both looked up and Trista froze.

'Oh, no. Joanne!' she exclaimed, and turned to the open door, racing up the stairs.

The kitchen light was burning and for a

moment Trista thought the room was empty, then a low moan had her racing around the table and the fallen chair. Joanne lay slumped on the floor, her face ashen, beads of moisture running off her forehead. Before Trista could bend down Dylan had thrust her to one side.

'Ring the ambulance,' he ordered, and began to run experienced hands over Joanne's body.

'But——'

'Do as I say, Tris.' His tone brooked no argument and she reached for the phone, her fingers shaking as she dialled the emergency number.

'They're on their way,' she whispered as she knelt down on the floor beside them.

Dylan had folded his jacket into a pillow and placed it beneath Joanne's head and he was taking her pulse. Joanne moaned softly and opened her eyes.

'Oh, Tris.' She grabbed for Trista's hand and clasped it tightly. 'Thank God! I was coming through to call you, but I didn't make it to the phone.'

'Just lie quietly, Joanne.' Dylan's voice had a soothing authority. 'How long have you been having the pains?'

'On and off all afternoon,' she replied weakly, her hand tightening on Trista's as another pain racked her. 'They went away for a while and then came back worse than before.'

Dylan ran his hands over Joanne's stomach and Trista watched him in surprise.

'Dylan——' she began uneasily.

'It's okay, Tris. I guess this is the time to come clean,' he said, looking straight at her. 'I never wanted to be a fisherman because I wanted to study medicine, which I did, so I do know what I'm doing. I'm a doctor, an obstetrician.'

'A doctor?' she repeated quietly, hardly able to take it in. She sat back on her heels.

Joanne smiled faintly. 'Then I'm in good hands.' She laughed tiredly. 'You never did look like a fisherman to me!'

A siren whirred as it approached the house.

'And here come more good hands.' Dylan smiled down at her. 'We'll have you at the hospital in no time. Tris, what's Joanne's doctor's number? I'll have to call him.'

Everything moved in a state of smooth precision. Dylan accompanied Joanne in the ambulance while Trista followed in her car. She moved in a state of dazed acceptance, and it wasn't until the first streaks of dawn began to wash the sky that she eventually climbed into bed.

Dylan assisted Dr Rivers, and Amy Elizabeth Vaughan, weighing in at five pounds, entered the world and left no one in any doubt that she was going to make her mark on it. Trista radioed Ray on board the *Blue Dancer* and he would be back in port before lunch.

Trista drove Dylan home in silence and when she drew up in the driveway and climbed out of the car she turned towards him. There was so much to say and she was at a loss to know where to start. However, Dylan spoke before she could make a comment.

'Get some sleep, Tris. I'll see you later.' And he walked off and left her.

Three days later she still hadn't heard from

him and she sank into a weary depression. It was all she could do to put on a cheerful front when she visited her sister-in-law. At least Joanne and the baby were progressing well and Ray was tickled pink with both of them.

On Thursday evening after visiting hours Ray tapped on the door of her flat.

'Okay, Tris, let's talk about it,' he said without preamble, sitting himself down at the kitchen table.

'About what?' Her eyes fell away from him.

'About what's troubling you.'

'Nothing's troubling me. I guess I'm just tired. It's been something of a chaotic week.'

'It's you and Dylan, isn't it?' Ray held up his hand when she would have made a denial. 'Let me finish, Tris. Joanne said she heard you arguing the night Amy was born.'

Tears welled in her eyes and she couldn't hold them back. 'Oh, Ray, I love him so much!'

Ray stood up and put his arms around her, holding her the way he had when she was a little girl.

'He asked me to marry him and I want to so much, but I can't. I can't!' she sobbed.

'Come on, love, dry your eyes. We need to get a few things sorted out.' Ray put her into a chair and sat down beside her.

'I went over to see Dylan today to thank him for what he did for Joanne and—well, to cut a long story short, he denied having had any relationship with our mother.'

'He denied it?' Trista repeated, and couldn't subdue the ray of hope that gleamed deep inside her. 'You mean . . . Oh, Ray!' her voice broke.

'So I decided the time had come to clear it all up once and for all.' Ray paused. 'So I rang her.'

Trista stared at him open-mouthed.

'I've always known where she was, ever since she came back that time,' he explained.

'You spoke to her?'

Ray nodded. 'She was surprised to hear from me.' he grimaced. 'Anyway, she told me the whole story. It wasn't Dylan. There was never anything between them. She left with Pete. She followed him to Adelaide and then they went to the States together when he took up that scholarship. They were still together when he was killed. That's when she came home. She said,' Ray looked down at his hands, 'that Pete was the only man she'd ever loved.'

'Oh, Ray!' Trista put her head on her arms and cried. 'All this time we've blamed Dylan. How can we tell him how wrong we've been, how wrong everyone's been?'

'I've told him already. We sorted it all out this morning.'

'What must he think of us?'

Ray shrugged and smiled at her. 'I don't know about me, but I've got a pretty fair idea what he thinks of you. I've never seen a guy so smitten. Though come to think of it, he always did have a soft spot for you. Whenever you wanted to come anywhere with us it was always Dylan who relented and let you come.'

He passed her his handkerchief to dry her eyes. 'So I suggest you go and see him tomorrow after work. You just might be able to work something out to your mutual advantage,' he laughed.

The hours seemed to drag next day and Trista went about her work on tenterhooks. When she was ready to walk across the road to his house she was as nervous as a kitten and her stomach churned. His car was in the driveway, and she walked on unsteady legs up the steps to knock on the open kitchen door.

'Hello, Trista,' Jean Parker greeted her from the table where she was preparing vegetables for their meal. 'Come on in. How's the new baby?'

'She's fine. I . . . I was looking for Dylan,' she got out breathily.

'He's gone down to the shore for a walk. He left about—oh, fifteen minutes ago. He shouldn't be long.'

'Oh.' Trista's heart sank.

'I think he said he was going down to Snapper Rock. You could always walk on down and meet him there,' Dylan's aunt suggested, a hint of a knowing smile lighting her face.

'Yes, I guess I could do that.' Trista turned to the door. 'I think I will. 'Bye for now.'

The sea was blue and chopped up by the breeze that whipped through her hair as she turned down the last part of the gravel track. He was standing in roughly the same place as she had been standing when she first saw him, and she stopped, her heart contracting painfully, her eyes moving over his tall broad figure.

He shifted his weight from one foot to the other and shoved his hands in his pockets. Trista took a deep breath and walked up to him.

'Hello,' she said, and his head snapped around to look at her. 'Your aunt said I'd find you here.'

His face looked drawn and tired and she gave him a nervous smile. When he remained silent she bit her lip.

'I wanted to talk to you. About . . . Ray told me about your brother and our mother and I wanted to apologise for thinking it was . . . it was you,' she finished lamely.

'There's no need for apologies. From all accounts it was something the whole town believed. What was it Ray said they called it? The Ashby Affair.' He gave a short laugh.

'But I . . .' Trista stopped, her heart sinking at the closed expression on his face.

'Perhaps I should be apologising to you, for Pete,' he said bitterly. 'You know, I somehow thought because you didn't mention her that your mother had died. I never even suspected she'd gone off with my brother. And he never mentioned her to me in the letters I got from him. He said he'd found someone, his lady he called her, and that they planned to marry when her divorce came through, but I just assumed she was an American he'd met over there. If it's any consolation, Trista, judging by his letters it was the real thing for him.'

'Ray said our mother told him she felt the same about Pete. I think perhaps I can understand a little better now how she felt, now that I——' She stopped and her eyes fell from his. 'Dylan, in the beginnning when you asked me if I remembered you and I denied that I did—well, it wasn't strictly true. I suppose, because of what everyone said about you and my mother, I kind of blotted you out of my mind. But I did remember breaking my arm and I did remember it was you who carried me up to the house.'

He smiled crookedly. 'That incident sticks in my memory, too. I felt so helpless. I hadn't a clue how to ease your pain. That's when I started to consider medicine. It was the first step for me.' He looked back over the bay. 'I couldn't forget the blind faith you had in me in those days. That's what I meant when we were making love when I said you reminded me of someone. You had damn near the same expression in your eyes then, and I didn't want to take advantage of that trust, Tris.'

'I'm sorry. I completely took the wrong end of the stick,' she said softly, and he shrugged. 'I thought you didn't want to make love to me because you were remembering my mother.'

'Didn't want to make love to you?' he repeated with feeling. 'My God, you don't know how hard it was to walk away and not make love to you!'

His words lit a blaze inside Trista, but she quelled the urge to touch him. They needed this time to talk, lay the misunderstandings.

'And your father didn't want you to be a doctor?' she prompted.

'To say the least!' he said wryly. 'That's why I left Lincoln. In the final blow-up that day he told me I took over the *Blue Dancer* or I got out. So I went. I used the money my mother left me to help put me through my studies. I was young and hot-headed. Today I may have done things differently, I don't know.' He sighed. 'But I do know I would have made a pretty rotten fisherman!'

They fell silent and Trista swallowed nervously. It was now or never. She had to say it now before she lost her nerve, and she was so close to doing that as all her uncertainty, all her mistrust, welled up inside her.

'Dylan, I love you. If ... if that offer still stands ...' Her voice faltered as he turned away from her his face bleak.

'It's no good, Tris. It would always be there, the talk, the ill-feeling.'

'Dylan, that doesn't matter, none of it matters. I was a fool to think it did,' she appealed to him, her hand going out to touch his arm.

'Tris, please!' He moved out of her reach. 'Do you think I want it this way?'

'Dylan?' Trista swallowed a rush of tears. 'Remember when I broke my arm? It was painful and you ... you kissed it better for me. Well, if I have to live without you then that pain will be an agony far greater than any I've experienced before. This week has shown me that,' she finished quietly.

He stood rigidly, tense and unbending.

'It hurts now, and,' she stepped close to him wanting to touch him again but so terribly afraid, 'if you could just kiss——' Her voice broke.

He turned then, his hands reaching out for her, pulling her into his arms, and she buried her face in the curve of his shoulder, tears of relief dampening his shirt.

'Oh, Tris,' he breathed thickly against her hair 'I can't let you go. Lord knows, I never wanted to.'

His hands cupped her face and his eyes burned down into hers. Then he was kissing her hungrily and she clung to him, returning his kisses with a passion that matched his own.

He sat down on the grassy verge, pulling her with him, and it was some time before either of them spoke.

'Well, my love, how's that pain now?' he asked a trifle unevenly.

Trista gave a joyous laugh, touching his lips gently with her finger. 'Another miraculous cure, Dr Ashby,' she said huskily, and he covered her fingers with his, placing a reverent kiss in her palm.

'About the doctor bit, Tris. I'm sorry I didn't mention it to you. I didn't intend that it become a secret, but when I came home it was to be a breathing space, a time to decide what I wanted to do with my future.' He grinned crookedly, the light of love still blazing in his eyes. 'I didn't know I'd meet the woman I'd been waiting for all my life!'

Trista turned her fingers in his hand so they twined with his.

'I'd been totally disillusioned with myself and my profession,' he continued. 'You see, there was this little boy in Brisbane who had a rare blood disease. He was six years old, a beaut little fellow, and we really fought for that kid, no harder than he fought himself, believe me, and we thought we'd won. Then he slipped away from us. It hit me, Tris, and I started asking myself, what's the use?' He paused.

'The letter about Dad's will came at an opportune time and I decided if I came back, had a go on the boat, I might be able to get everything back into perspective.'

'And have you decided?' Trista asked softly.

He nodded. 'Joanne and little Amy restored my dented faith. But I guess I knew all along. I just needed to prove I was right. I'd never have made a fisherman like my father and Ray. That's why

I'm going ahead and selling Ray the *Blue Dancer*. So, do you think you can take being married to a doctor? I promise to do you a special cut rate when you have our kids.' He grinned.

'Oh, Dylan, I love you!' She wound her arms around his neck and smiled up at him. 'I accept.'

Dylan wasted no time kissing her for good measure. 'Mmm, you feel so good in my arms,' he murmured huskily as his lips claimed hers again.

As he raised his head a battered utility turned into sight, heading for the boat ramp. Trista went to draw away from him, but he held her fast.

'Shall we provide more food for the gossips? Let's start a brand new Ashby affair.' His eyes held hers. 'A real affair. One I promise will last for the rest of our lives.'

Harlequin Plus
A WORD ABOUT THE AUTHOR

Australian author Lynsey Stevens has a quality that everyone loves in a person, and few can resist in a writer: a sense of humor. Of herself, she cheerfully says, "Although I'm not an oil painting, I make up for it by being 'a very nice person' with a 'scintillating personality.'"

Lynsey's days are spent at a job she thoroughly enjoys. She is a librarian who engages in all sorts of professional activities related to books, though her first love is her writing.

She began with attempts at historical romance, progressed to adventure and espionage and even tried her hand at what she calls "sexy stories"—from which she claims to have gained her expertise at the "steamy" scenes in her present books.

Her first romance novel was not as readily accepted for publication as she had expected – in fact, it was rejected. But undaunted, spunky Lynsey kept at it, and she now has several published books to her credit.

As to real-life romance, she hints at the presence of a Harlequin hero in her life, but swears he's just a good friend—though she does admit she's not the type to kiss and tell under any circumstances!

4 FREE
Harlequin Romances